ICEPICK

A Selection of Titles by Phillip DePoy

The Foggy Moscowitz Series

COLD FLORIDA *
THREE SHOT BURST *

The Fever Devilin Series

THE DEVIL'S HEARTH
THE WITCH'S GRAVE
A MINISTER'S GHOST
A WIDOW'S CURSE
THE DRIFTER'S WHEEL
A CORPSE'S NIGHTMARE
DECEMBER'S THORN

* *available from Severn House*

ICEPICK

The Foggy Moscowitz Series

Phillip DePoy

This first world edition published 2018
in Great Britain and the USA by
SEVERN HOUSE PUBLISHERS LTD of
Eardley House, 4 Uxbridge Street, London W8 7SY.
Trade paperback edition first published
in Great Britain and the USA 2018 by
SEVERN HOUSE PUBLISHERS LTD.

British Library Cataloguing in Publication Data
A CIP catalogue record for this title is available from the British Library.

ISBN-13: 978-0-7278-8795-5 (cased)
ISBN-13: 978-1-84751-923-8 (trade paper)
ISBN-13: 978-1-78010-979-4 (e-book)

All Severn House titles are printed on acid-free paper.

Severn House Publishers support the Forest Stewardship Council™ [FSC™],
the leading international forest certification organisation.
All our titles that are printed on FSC certified paper carry the FSC logo.

Typeset by Palimpsest Book Production Ltd.,
Falkirk, Stirlingshire, Scotland.
Printed and bound in Great Britain by
TJ International, Padstow, Cornwall.

ONE

Florida, 1976

S ammy 'Icepick' Franks drove his snappy black Lincoln town car up to the docks around three in the morning. He got out, smoked half a Swisher Sweet, and dragged a dead body out of his trunk. He shot a dog to keep it quiet, which is a window on Icepick's personality. Someone heard the shot and called the cops. Still, Icepick managed to dump the body into the bay and scamper out of town before any of the local constabulary showed up. That's how it was in Fry's Bay, Florida. You wanted *fast*? Call for a hooker. You wanted *stupid*, Officer Brady was your man.

Ordinarily I wouldn't have been made aware of such goings-on, since I worked for Child Protective Services. The dead body was a full-grown man, and the dog was dead. But Brady was a new man in town, so I listened as patiently as I could when he called some time after four that morning.

'So why call me, Officer?' I didn't even sit up in bed. 'About the dog: call the Humane Society. About the stiff: call the coroner. How is any of this my problem?'

'Oh, it involves you, Moscowitz,' Brady sneered into the phone.

'So, tell me how,' I said.

'Eyewitnesses are kids,' he told me. 'They're the ones who put in the call after the assailant shot the dog. They went out to see what had happened, and saw the floater.'

'Who are they?' I sat up. 'They live near the docks?'

'No. Some little *wigwam* vagrants, sleeping near the old abandoned bakery over here on Blake Road.'

'You mean Seminole children?'

'Yeah. On Blake Road.'

* * *

Nobody lived on Blake. It was odd to have an orphan alley like it in the middle of town. Not much of a road at all, really. Only a block long. The air was lonely and the storefronts were always cold. I never knew Florida could be so cold before I came here from Brooklyn. But with Blake Road, it wasn't so much the temperature. It was more the way a tombstone feels, or the sound of a late-night train.

In my line of work, I was used to the midnight call. Child Protective Services was a new deal and people still weren't sure what I did, but they didn't mind calling me at all hours. The name seemed perfectly explanatory to me: I was supposed to protect children. That was my service. Still, I got the occasional call about adoptions. Sometimes parents would ring me up to discipline their children. Once a guy came into my office and asked me if I would show him photos of the children I'd worked with. I got him out of my office right away, and then went home to take a shower.

But this particular night, there I was at the docks, standing next to a police car, blinking. I had on the nice, gabardine salt-and-pepper suit, a hand-me-down from my Uncle Red in Brooklyn. Brady was in a navy-blue Sears ready-to-wear that looked like he never took it off.

'And where are these alleged children now?' I asked Brady.

'Come on.' He sighed and we headed over to Blake Road, past the empty buildings.

Brady opened the door and he stood there like a doorman. 'After you.'

The place was dark despite three candles, and it smelled like mold. It was littered with rotted cardboard boxes and heaps of paper.

I took a gander around. Then, in the flickering light, a young boy appeared, maybe eight, Seminole, calm. Right beside him was a girl, a little older, holding a very long knife. It was a cold night and they weren't dressed warmly enough: jeans, T-shirts, sneakers.

Thing was, unaccompanied children wandering around after midnight – it just wasn't something you'd see so often in Fry's Bay. So, I had to ask, 'Aren't you kids out a little late? Won't your parents be worried?'

Before either of the kids could say anything, Brady took out his pistol. And there was another guy with him all of a sudden. I'd seen him before, but I couldn't remember his name. 'What the hell do you think you're doing with that gun?' I snapped at Brady. 'I realize you're new in town, so I'll explain slow. These kids need to be drinking hot cocoa. Calling their parents. Last thing they need is some fat cop with a heater in his hand!'

'Hello, Foggy,' the other cop said, the one *without* a gun.

Then I remembered. His name was Watkins. He was a pretty good guy.

'Get your pal to back away, please, Officer,' I said to Watkins.

'The little piece of crap has a knife,' Brady hissed. 'That's why I let you come in first. When I tried to take her into custody earlier, she pulled it on me!'

It was a big knife. Looked like a broadsword in her little hand.

But I had to smile. 'Yeah, I can see how a grown man with a handgun might be paralyzed by a small child with a kitchen utensil. And you only outweigh her by about three hundred pounds.'

'Look, Jew-boy,' Brady snapped, 'I'd just as soon shoot this little *wigwam* in the head, do the town a favor. They're like roaches.'

I got in between him and the kids instantly.

'First try to shoot *me*,' I told him. 'Let's see how that works out for you.'

Watkins sighed.

'Could we conclude this little scuffle with Child Protective Services, Officer Brady?' he suggested. 'Put your weapon away, OK?'

'Not likely,' Brady said, his gun right in my belly.

I stared him in the eye so hard it hurt the back of his brain. I could tell because he twitched.

'You called me,' I said to him calmly. 'What did you think I was going to do? My job is to be on the side of the child. Hence the name "Child *Protective* Services", Officer Brady.'

Without waiting for any sort of answer from Brady, I turned to face the kids.

'I'm not from Florida, myself,' I said to the girl, 'so I came here with a lot of preconceptions about what it would be like. For instance, I originally figured it never got cold in Florida. But a night like this? With a fog from the docks? I shiver just looking out the window at it. So, how about we go someplace warmer? I don't want to catch a chill.'

The girl blinked. Her eyes flashed toward the cops, and then she looked right back at me. That's all. No talk.

'They don't speak no English, looks like,' Brady observed.

'Maybe you'd like a shot of Scotch?' I suggested to her.

The very merest hint of a smile touched the corners of her mouth. She understood English.

'And as to that knife,' I went on, 'it looks very much like one that Dan Red Bear carries – to kill alligators, he says. Only his is not quite so clean. And yours has been sharpened recently, so I can see it's taken care of. Red Bear, he's a good guy, but, you know, a little lazy, wouldn't you say?'

That gave them both a smile. A little one.

I glanced at the boy, and then asked the girl in the Seminole language: '*Chatsosi?*'

She seemed surprised that I knew the word for *younger brother*.

'*Hum-bux-tchay?*' I went on. I was pretty sure that was the word for *eat*.

'Ho!' the boy answered quickly, nodding.

'Ssh!' the girl told him instantly.

'What the hell are you talking about?' Brady mumbled.

'I have established that they are brother and sister,' I answered, smiling at the girl, 'and that they're hungry.'

'*Efa,*' the girl snapped, glaring at Brady.

I nodded.

'What did she call me?' Brady demanded.

'*Esticha-bucke-nawhansle,*' I told the girl.

She nodded.

'Moscowitz?' Brady snarled.

'She called you a dog and I corrected her,' I told him. 'I told her you just weren't very good at being a man.'

Watkins laughed.

'*Cheh ma solehta estoma cheh?*' I asked the girl.

She didn't answer.

'OK then, it doesn't matter how old you are,' I told her, 'my name is Foggy Moscowitz, and I'm the guy who helps you. I work for this county's Child Protective Services. See?'

I showed her my badge.

'I know.' She squinted. 'John Horse told us about you.'

I was happy to hear her mention John Horse – a Seminole legend. I'd been around him a lot, but even so, I wasn't sure he was completely real. I was also a bit perplexed by her mention of his name.

'John Horse.' I stared at the kid, a little suspiciously. 'You want me to try to get in touch with him?'

She shook her head, but she put her knife away. Tucked it back in some sort of holster she had tied behind her back.

'All right.' I shrugged. 'What now?'

'We'll go with you,' she said to me in no uncertain terms. 'Not them.'

I turned to face the constabulary.

'Gents,' I announced, 'looks like I'll take it from here.'

Watkins nodded. Brady wouldn't budge.

'Nothing doing,' he objected. 'The girl threatened a police officer, and they're both vagrants.'

'No,' I shot back. 'A vagrant has no fixed abode and no visible means of support. One, these kids live in the Seminole town in the swamp where the legendary John Horse lives. Two, you are currently looking at their means of support, which is me. Am I invisible to you? And finally, City Ordinance 213-A provides any material witness to a crime, which they are, with counsel. You want me for your counsel, kids?'

'Absolutely,' the girl answered instantly.

'What makes you think they live in the swamp?' Brady began, irritated.

'The knife, the accent, and a pretty good guess,' I snapped, 'but if you're in doubt, let's ask them about that too.'

I spun around.

'Do you or do you not live in the town established by John Horse?' I asked them both.

'We do,' the girl answered, defiant of the man with his gun pointed at her.

'And do you consider yourselves to be wards of my office? Say *yes*.'

She glanced at me, then back at the cop.

'Yes,' she said, even louder.

I turned back around. 'There you have it.'

'Come on, Brady,' Watkins complained. 'Let Foggy take the kids. You and me, we'll go get some coffee and run the license plate the kid gave us, right?'

'She pulled a knife!' Brady seethed. 'I think I'll just shoot her in the leg and call it self-defense!'

He aimed his pistol.

Before he knew what hit him, I took one step forward and stomped Brady's instep. On the upswing of that same foot I cracked his shin. Then I twisted his pistol arm up and away; wrenched his muscles. The guy yelped like a dog.

In the next second I had his gun, a regulation revolver, and he was about to fall over. I snapped open the weapon, emptied the core and the chamber, and handed it to Watkins. Brady started really feeling the pain in his foot at that point. He lost his balance and sat down, cursing.

I shook my head.

'I'm filing charges against this moron first thing in the morning,' I told Watkins. 'Obstructing an officer of the court in the performance of his duties and illegal threats against a juvenile ward of CPS with a police firearm. You don't have to worry about agreeing with me, Watkins. Yudda's standing in the doorway. He'll corroborate.'

At that moment Yudda, the town's finest seafood chef and a man whose insomnia rivaled my own, stepped out of the darkness. He wore his typical black beret, greasy apron, and dime store flip-flops, even on a chilly night.

'I saw the whole thing, Officer,' he yawned, completely emotionless. 'That fat policeman sitting on the ground there, he threatened those children and – and an officer of the court named Moscowitz – with his police weapon. He then refused to lower said weapon in the presence of the presiding authority for said children, regarding Local Statute 189-A, section 11. Right?'

'Perfect,' I answered.

'Can I go now?' he complained. '*Casablanca* is on the late-late.'

'Thanks, Yudda,' I called out. 'See you for lunch.'

'Got a good feeling about the morning catch,' he said, ambling away. 'I think it might be skate wing.'

I glanced down at Brady. 'You should try his skate wing. It's the best in the state. And, as I was saying, I'm filing charges against you in the morning, with a third-party witness.'

'What made you bring Yudda with you, Foggy?' Watkins asked me.

'Me?' I smiled innocently. 'I think Yudda probably just happened to be walking by. He has insomnia. He likes to walk around at night coming up with ideas for tomorrow's menu.'

'You sonofabitch,' Brady snarled. 'I'm the law. I'll come after you so fast you won't know what hit you. You'll be sorry about this. *Very* sorry.'

I could tell that he meant it. He was out for blood.

Still, I took a step closer to him. 'You point a gun at me again, you'd better use it. And if you ever call this girl a "wigwam" again, I'll crack your nuts open.'

He glared up at me. 'What?'

'I'm taking the kids to my place,' I said. 'I happen to have hot cocoa for just such occasions.'

'What about the Scotch?' the girl muttered, throwing a little grin my way.

'That's what I'm having, you delinquent,' I told her.

She took her brother's hand.

'You speak the people's language with a funny accent,' she told me as we headed out of the alley and on to the street.

'What do you want from me?' I asked her. 'I speak English, Yiddish, and Hebrew – *everything's* got a funny accent.'

'You're a Jew.'

'Technically,' I agreed.

'I always wanted to meet one. John Horse told me that we're related – your tribe and mine. You are the tribes from across the ocean, and we are the tribes from this continent.'

'John Horse told you – I told *him* that! He's stealing my material!'

She nodded solemnly. 'Oh. Well. He does that. He's not afraid to admit it.'

I stared down at her.

'Do you know what the word *precocious* means?' I asked her.

'Is it a Jewish word?' she asked me.

'Well,' I said, heading toward my little apartment with an ocean view, 'we may have invented the concept, now that you mention it.'

TWO

My place was very neat for a person such as myself. I kept it orderly just in case I happened to bring home a date. Most of the women I knew were impressed with a clean home. It looked like this: you walk in the front door, and you see a nice living room. To the left there's the kitchen, to the right, a Spartan boudoir. The best part is that practically the whole back wall is sliding glass doors with a view of the ocean you wouldn't believe.

It was a clear night, and the moon was high, so the light on the water was just about as silver as you could get, and the rolling waves looked like liquid shadows.

The kids stood in the doorway. I got the impression they were afraid to go in.

'What's the hold up?' I asked, standing behind them.

'It's very nice,' the girl whispered.

'I'm afraid I'll break something,' the boy said, even softer.

I understood. I remembered John Horse's house in the swamp land. It was made of cinder blocks and had a dirt floor. It was poorly lit by a single oil lamp. There was a beat-up old chair that a junkyard wouldn't take, a dining table that wasn't much better, and various spooky paraphernalia. On the floor next to his dining table was a two-burner Sterno hot plate. There was nothing on the walls – it was all bare concrete block. There was one window in each wall except for the one with the door. That was it.

And his house was the nicest one in the village.

I ushered them past the threshold and closed the door behind me.

'Not to worry.' I pointed to the 1930s couch. 'Sit.'

'It looks like a movie set,' the girl said, staring at the couch.

'Thrift store,' I explained, heading for the kitchen.

Ten minutes later we were all sitting in the living room and drinking. They were on the couch with hot chocolate. I was in an overstuffed chair finishing my first Scotch, my feet up on the coffee table.

I hadn't asked them a single question. A kid will talk when a kid is ready. I drank.

At last the girl set down her mug, careful to put a coaster under it – yes, I had coasters – and cleared her throat.

I didn't respond.

'Your name is Foggy.' She wasn't looking at me. She was looking down at her hands.

'Yes.' I sipped.

'What kind of a name is that? Is it a Jewish name?'

'It's more of a pejorative descriptor,' I answered her. 'I pretended to be confused a lot when I was younger.'

'Why?' She looked up at me.

'Why?' I tossed back what was left of my Scotch. 'The last thing you wanted to be was smart in an enclave of hoodlums and wise guys such as comprised my boyhood cohorts in Brooklyn.'

She sighed. 'I know what most of those words mean,' she said, 'and I appreciate that you're talking to me like I'm an adult. But you speak your own language with a funny accent too, and maybe you use words to trick people just as much as you use them to talk.'

I nodded. '*Precocious* means that you're mentally advanced for your age, which is what you are. You just proved that.'

'Oh.' She sat back.

I glanced over at the younger brother. His eyelids were heavy, and he was about to drop his cocoa.

'Maybe your brother would like to go to sleep now,' I suggested. 'He can camp out on the sofa. I got a sleeping bag or two.'

'*Catsha Tuste-Nuggee!*' she said sharply to her brother.

He snapped awake, eyes wide.

'Wait,' I told her slowly. 'I think I know what some of that means. His name is *Little Cloud*?'

'Yes,' she said.

'I would like to go to sleep now,' Little Cloud said.

I was up in a flash, into my bedroom and back without a word, delivering two sleeping bags. One was black and half-sized, perfect for the boy. The other one was an adult bag with some sort of crazy pattern on it.

I tossed the black one to Little Cloud.

'Crawl in,' I told him. 'We'll worry about brushing your teeth and everything else, like, tomorrow, OK?'

He smiled. 'OK.'

He was inside the bag and out like a light two minutes later.

The girl and I went into the kitchen. She sat on the counter and I got a good look at her for the first time. Her face was oddly shaped and her eyes didn't look like they belonged to a child. Her T-shirt said FLORIDA PANTHERS in all capitals across the front of it, and her sneakers were a size too big: thrift store or donated clothes, I figured. She had no coat, as I may have mentioned, on a very chilly night.

I poured another Scotch.

'Florida Panthers,' I said, nodding toward her shirt. 'That's, like, a joke, right? A hockey team in Florida?'

She shrugged.

'OK – you want something to eat?' I asked her.

She shook her head.

'Why did you ask me about my name?' I wondered, not looking at her.

'You can't trust a person if you don't know what that person's name means,' she said.

'You don't want me to trust you, then.'

She nodded.

'I don't know who you are yet,' she told me.

'I'm the director of Child Protective Services for the county of—'

'Not your job,' she interrupted. 'Who you *are*.'

'Ah. That.' I took a healthy slug of Scotch. 'Well, I am a Jewish car thief from Brooklyn. I was responsible for something bad happening to a kid, a baby, about five years ago. I took it on the lam and ended up here. Then God, who is certainly a very strange comedian, set me up here in Fry's Bay protecting children. From people like me. Enough, or do you want more details?'

'It's enough for now.' She looked me in the eye. 'My name is *Topalargee*.'

'I don't know that word. Do you know what it means in English?'

'*The Wonder*,' she said plainly.

'And you are named that because . . .?'

'John Horse named me that,' she answered, 'when he found out that I could read other people's thoughts.'

'Sorry?'

'I can read minds. For example: you stole some woman's car, in Brooklyn, but she'd left her baby in the back seat. She chased after you and died. You made the baby an orphan. And your people, I mean whites, they don't take care of orphans the way human beings do. You feel guilty. *That's* why you do the work you do.'

I stared at her for what seemed like a long time, then smiled.

'John Horse told you all that.' I knew because I had told John Horse all that.

She looked down with a little smile of her own. 'Yes. But it would have been a good trick.'

'Had me going for a minute.'

'Usually works on whites.' She shrugged. 'I actually got my name because I was born dead but came alive after a few minutes. I was named Topalargee right away.'

'Good.' I finished the Scotch and set the glass on the counter beside her. 'Tell me what you're doing in Fry's Bay in the middle of the night with a little brother and a big knife.'

'Our mother didn't come home,' she said right away, 'so we came looking for her.'

'Your mother – what? Works here in town?'

'For the hotel. She works there, cleaning rooms.'

'You mean the Benton Inn or the Flamingo Motel?'

'Benton,' she said, glaring at me. 'The Flamingo stinks.'

'Right. Your mother didn't come home tonight and—'

'Three nights ago,' she corrected.

'She's been gone three nights? Is that normal?'

'No,' she explained. 'She sleeps in town sometimes, at the Benton, if it's too late to walk home. But not three nights in a row.'

'She walks to your house from the Benton?' I shook my head. 'That's, like, ten miles.'

'Seven,' she told me. 'Takes her about two hours.'

'Yeah,' I sighed, 'I wouldn't want to walk through the swamp that time of the night. But three days is a while. So you came to town with your brother.'

'He wouldn't stay home. He kind of insisted on coming with me. He thinks he's being protective.' She was trying to seem tolerant, but it sounded an awful lot like being proud.

'And you both . . . what? I assume you went to the Benton first.'

She nodded. 'They said she hadn't come to work in two days.'

I was beginning to admire the kid's stoicism. Most people her age would have been a mess. She was a rock.

'So, you went looking . . . just in general?'

'No. I went to the room where she usually sleeps when she stays at the inn. All of her stuff was still there.'

'Stuff?'

'Walking clothes and shoes, tribal necklace, pictures of me and my brother.'

'It was all still in her room.' I nodded. 'She's somewhere still dressed in her fancy hotel uniform. That's a suit coat and dress, probably heels, right?'

She nodded.

'What were you doing over there on Blake Road?'

'Following the trail.'

'Trail?' I asked her.

'My mother left a trail, Foggy,' she said, still without a trace of panic. 'I don't know why. We were following it.'

'What kind of trail?'

'Markings. We lost it, though. If it was in the swamp, we'd probably be all right. But town is confusing.'

Then, before she could stop herself, she yawned.

'OK,' I said, concluding our little tête-à-tête, 'time for you to visit dreamland and me to finish my own sleep routine which you so rudely interrupted.'

'No,' she said immediately, 'we have to go back out to pick up the trail.'

'Not tonight,' I interrupted firmly. 'We catch a few Zs so we're worth a dime, and we're up with the sun, right? Then we go back over to Blake Road, and we find your mother before lunchtime!'

She tried to object, but she yawned again instead.

'Yeah,' I told her, 'hop down. Sleeping bag.'

Against her will, she knew I was right. She slid off the countertop and made her way into the sleeping bag. After a minute, her breathing sounded like she was asleep. But just in case, I locked all my doors from the inside with a key that I hid in my bedroom. I couldn't have her slipping out in the middle of the night, which is exactly what I would have done if I'd been in her oversized shoes.

THREE

The sun was a very rude alarm clock. I'd deliberately left my curtains open so that it would get me up, but I objected to the amount of joy it got out of waking me. In other words, it was a very beautiful morning.

I had my clothes on and my tie halfway tied before I heard a ruckus at the door. The girl was trying to bust out, her big old knife strapped to her back like a sword.

'Hey, Wonder Girl,' I called out. 'The door's locked from the inside. Give it a break. We're going out in about five, so why don't you help yourself to some juice or whatever it is you like to have in the morning when you wake up.'

'I've been awake for an hour,' she grumbled, 'and I usually like to kill a chicken and eat its raw carcass for breakfast.'

'No,' her brother corrected from inside his sleeping bag. 'She likes Cheerios.'

'Oh.' I ambled in the direction of the kitchen. 'Well, I have neither a live chicken nor said cereal. How about some toast?'

'Are you circumcised?' She stared at me.

'Cut it out!' I'm pretty sure I scowled at her, which would have been unlike me to do, but she was provoking me.

'She's just mad,' the boy, Little Cloud said, stretching, 'because she thinks we ought to be out looking already, not eating breakfast. When she's mad, she tries to irritate people. I hate it.'

'Yeah,' I conceded, 'but I would probably irritate a lot of people if my mother was missing.'

Half an hour later the three of us were in the cold shadows of the building near the abandoned bakery on Blake Road, the place where the kids had holed up the night before. It was hard to see anything. I leaned in close to the wall. I knelt and examined the floor. Just as I was about to give up, I saw it.

I stood.

'What's your mother's name?' I asked. 'Does it have something to do with water?'

'Why do you want to know?' Wonder Girl folded her arms.

I pointed to a place on the wall. There was a quick image scraped there, maybe by a nail, that looked very much like a snake and waves.

'*Echu Matta* is her name,' Little Cloud told me.

'It means *Water Serpent*,' I said.

What we didn't talk about was the smear of blood, relatively fresh, right next to the picture.

'She was here, your mother,' I went on. 'That's her doing.'

Little Cloud nodded. 'It's the last thing we found last night, before the gunshot and the dead body in the bay.'

'Didn't think you would see it,' the girl added.

You had to admire the kids: lost a mother, heard a gunshot in the dead of the night, saw a body in the middle of the bay – and just as matter-of-fact as Brooklyn wise guys.

'So, all that brouhaha with Brady scotched your search,' I said.

Wonder Girl nodded.

I took a gander around the room. The smell was unpleasant, but the air of oppression was more significant. Something weird had happened there, and recently.

Then I caught sight of something in the shadows. Hard enough to see in the daylight; would have been invisible at night.

'And what about that mess?' I asked after a second.

Their eyes went to what I was staring at: two cans of Sterno and an overturned pot. Next to that there were four or five ratty pillows.

'Somebody stayed here,' I said, 'at least overnight.'

Fry's Bay was too small to have vagrants. Sometimes high school kids would squirrel into someplace like this, but it was mostly to make out or smoke weed. People had cooked here. People had slept here.

'You think my mother slept here?' Wonder Girl asked. 'Why would she do that?'

'Yeah,' I answered. 'Good question.'

The boy edged over to the pillows and began sniffing like a hound. He turned to his sister.

'She was here, though.' He pointed to one of the pillows. 'Put her head there.'

'We would have figured this out last night,' Wonder Girl said angrily, 'if it hadn't been for that dickweed Brady.'

'Let's think about this,' I ventured. 'Could she have been hiding out here? Maybe with some other people?'

'Hiding from who?' the girl snapped. 'And what other people?'

'Are there other Seminole women who work at the hotel?'

'Yes,' she answered slowly. 'And when we went there, I didn't see any of them.'

'Could be coincidence,' I told her. 'Could have been working in some other part of the place.'

'But.' She squinted.

'But,' I agreed.

'Don't you smell that?' the boy asked, shaking his head.

'That rotten cardboard smell?' I made a face.

'Fear,' he shot back. 'They were afraid, the people who stayed here. And they were mostly women. Only one man.'

I turned to the girl. 'Is he really this good?'

She nodded. 'He's the first person John Horse comes to for something like this.'

'Could he, like, track the smell?'

She looked at her brother.

'The problem is all the other smells,' he admitted. 'That cardboard smell, the rat shit, mold – very difficult.'

'OK then,' I told them both, 'let's look at it this way. If you had a couple of people you wanted to hide from the police and the general populace, you wouldn't go out of this dump that way, toward the main drag. You'd head up the alley. Toward the bakery.'

'Why not just stay here?' the girl asked.

'The storefronts on Blake Road get checked every once in a while, but the patrol guy never goes up the alley. Partly because it's too hard to turn the squad car around, and partly because the patrol guy might find kids up to mischief, and there goes his quiet night. He'd just as soon live and let live unless it was something really wild.'

'Meaning the bakery is a safer place to hide.' She looked

around. 'So why did they spend the night, or a couple of nights, here?'

'By me?' I gave them a little shrug. 'Indicates out-of-towners. Found an abandoned building, didn't know the score, stayed here until they saw the way the patrol cars operated, then moved.'

'To the bakery,' she said, heading out the door.

Her brother and I followed, up the alley toward the loading dock. The bay was down but there was a half-open regular door to one side.

The inside of the bakery was colder than New Jersey cement. The brick walls had moss and ice on them. The abandoned machines and conveyer belts looked like something out of a horror film in the dim light. High windows, nearly at the top of the thirty-foot walls, let in just enough morning light to confirm that the rest of the place was a crypt.

The floor of the open factory was littered with bird crap in layers and patterns like a Jackson Pollock. But there was a place untouched by such avian artistry: a large rectangle, about the size of a small mobile home. Beyond that, at the far end of the whole place, there was a rusted iron staircase that led up to a small, glass-faced office.

Little Cloud looked at the clean space on the floor.

'There was something here until last night,' he said softly.

'There was something there,' I agreed. 'You're sure it was that recent?'

He looked up at me. 'It was like a big truck.'

'Or a storage container that goes on a big truck,' I told him, 'and then maybe on to a train.'

He looked back down. 'Yes.'

'My brother has learned to follow trails better than anybody,' the girl said to me, 'but you're not half bad yourself.'

What I *thought* was that something very bad had happened to the kids' mother, something that involved being shipped in a storage container. But what I *said* to the girl was, 'Who taught him the tracking thing?'

'John Horse.' Her voice suddenly sounded strange to me.

John Horse again. He always claimed to be the region's oldest living Seminole citizen. Some people had told me that he *couldn't* die. Unless he just felt like it one day. He'd been around for a while, and he knew a lot. He wasn't a chief or anything, more like the village grandfather. He wouldn't ever tell anyone his real name, but apparently a long time ago people started calling him John Horse after another Seminole from a longer time ago. The old John Horse was a great leader, so at first our guy was called New John Horse. But since the old John Horse had been dead for more than a hundred years, most people dropped the 'New' and let it go at that. I had a lot of respect for the guy – a genuine rabbi if I ever saw one.

But something struck me as fishy about the number of times the kids had invoked his name in the short time I'd known them.

I folded my arms. 'We're going to have to get a little bit more honest with each other,' I said softly to them, 'or I'll just take you both to my office and we'll fill out paperwork all day.'

'What do you mean?' the girl asked.

'Stop it,' I told her. 'You know exactly what I mean. You didn't just show up in town last night. John Horse sent you here.'

It was a good guess. I could tell by the way they looked at each other that it was true.

'So, give,' I insisted. 'What's really going on?'

Before either one of them could answer, there was a noise in the upstairs office area. Without thinking I scooped up both kids, one under each arm, and we were hidden behind one of the machines in a tight second.

There were low voices. They were too far away and too well-insulated to hear clearly, but there was some sort of argument going on.

'Two men,' the boy said softly.

'Three,' I corrected. 'Maybe even four. Listen to the pattern, not the pitch.'

He listened. Then, eyes wider, he nodded. 'Four. Good.'

'Not my first time eavesdropping,' I whispered.

'Our mother really is missing,' Wonder Girl said very close to my ear. 'But we didn't come here on our own. John Horse sent us. He's in trouble, and the Panther clan needs our help.'

I vaguely remembered something about the various Seminole clans; Panther was John Horse's family, though the official lineage was matriarchal – like it was for my tribe.

I turned to look at her. 'Why are you telling me this now?' I asked her, looking her in the eye.

'You picked us up and carried us,' she answered simply, as if it were a complete answer.

'Yeah, all right.' I turned away again. 'You two stay put. I mean it. I'm going to get a little closer to the pageant.'

Without waiting for them to say anything, I stood and sauntered toward the iron staircase. No point in hiding and sneaking around. When you hide, people get the idea you're suspicious. When you're bold, they just think you're stupid.

'Hey!' I shouted out. 'What's going on up there?'

I figured if it was something truly bad, the guys who were arguing would want to be careful. And if it was nothing nefarious, they'd just be irritated.

But when I yelled, everything went silent, which told me what I wanted to know.

'I'm with the county,' I hollered. 'This is private property. You're in violation of Section Seven, part D. Come on down here with some ID, right away. Do it now; I'm in a hurry. I'm busy with more important stuff.'

In the first place, 'Section Seven' was completely made up, but in the second place, the overworked county employee was a good gambit. Every time I'd ever used it, some wise guy either wanted to pay me off or shoot me. Either way, I always found out what I wanted to know.

In this case, there was another moment of silence before a vaguely familiar voice finally answered. 'Moscowitz?' it sang out.

It only took me a second to register that the voice was Brady's, the cop who liked to point his gun at little kids.

So that didn't bode well, because he also liked to point his gun at me. And in the next second, Brady appeared at the top of the iron staircase, pistol in hand.

'Do you always have your gun out?' I asked him calmly. 'You're not worried that it's too . . . I don't know . . . Freudian?'

'What are you doing here?' he snarled.

'My job,' I snapped. 'You?'

He started down the stairs, gun aimed right at my chest, as far as I could tell.

'Clear out or get shot,' he said, nearing the bottom of the steps. 'I'm in the line of duty.'

'Me too, as I was saying,' I told him, actually taking a step closer to the gun, 'and, once again, like last night, I have back-up witnesses. They wish to remain anonymous for safety reasons, but they're here.'

That stopped him, at least for a second.

I kept my eyes on him but called out over my shoulder, 'Make some noise over there, would you, so this dickweed knows I'm serious.'

And instantly the kids banged on the conveyer belt apparatus. It was really loud. Brady almost dropped his toy.

Still, he kept himself together.

'I told you what would happen the next time I saw you,' he snarled, 'on account of stomping me down last night.'

'You might have said something about it *in your mind*,' I corrected, 'but all you said out loud was that I'd be sorry. And on that count, you were right. I'm very sorry to see you here today.'

'Then shove off,' he snapped. 'Get lost and stay there.'

'Not really,' I allowed. 'Seems the tykes you menaced last night were only here looking for their mother, who's gone missing. How's it going to look if I say in my report that you stopped me from finding somebody's lost mother?'

He took another step toward me.

'Who says you're going to be in any condition to write a report?' he wanted to know.

'Did you forget my witnesses?' I asked him.

'Shut up. It's them two wampum brats. That's who you got for witnesses.'

Before I could deny it, the girl stepped into the open.

'Right,' she told Officer Brady. 'I see you. I am a witness.'

It was such a weird, bold thing to do that it caught everyone off guard.

I recovered first. 'What do you think, Brady? You're going to shoot a little kid?'

Just then somebody from up in the office hollered, 'Brady! What's the racket?'

Brady stared me right in the eye.

'It's nothing; I'm taking care of it,' he called out. 'Everything's OK.'

I wasn't over being confused by that when Brady pulled off his next unexpected trick.

'Seriously, Moscowitz, take off,' he whispered. 'You're blowing the deal here.'

'I have no idea what you're talking about,' I answered, just as soft.

'If you ever want to find the kids' mother alive,' he told me, sounding just a little bit more like a human being, 'you'll give me a little room. I mean it.'

I don't know what made me take him seriously, but I did. Could have been the look in his eye, like we were sharing a secret. Could have been that he smiled at the kids in a very sympathetic way. Could have just been the fact that he didn't shoot me – always a good sign in any relationship.

Whatever the reason, I had an overwhelming intuition to trust him, despite my history with the guy. And intuition has always been a better friend to me than any person I ever knew. So, I backed away in the direction of the kids.

'No,' the girl said. 'We're not leaving.'

'I got a hunch,' I told her. 'We really ought to scram.'

The boy appeared. 'He's right.'

With that the boy headed toward the exit. Sighing, the girl followed.

'I'm going to want to know a whole lot more about this before sundown,' I whispered to Brady.

He put away his gun. 'Assuming we're both still alive by then.'

FOUR

I took the kids to Yudda's even though I knew he wasn't open yet. His place was on the edge of town, near the docks, close to the ocean but only about a five-minute walk from the abandoned bakery. The streets were warming up nicely, even though the sky was overcast. As we got closer to the joint, the smell of wood burning and some sort of serious spice – maybe fenugreek – filled the air.

'Curry,' I said out loud.

'Why did we leave?' the girl fumed.

'Listen, Wonder Girl—' I began.

'You know,' she interrupted, 'when white people translate our names into English, it sounds stupid. My name is *Topalargee*. What if, instead of *Foggy*, my people called you *Wet Mist*? Isn't that what *Foggy* means?'

I stopped walking. 'You've got a very good point. Never thought of it like that. Sorry. But, do you have a . . . what they call a *nickname*? Because Foggy is not my actual name, you understand. It's just what certain people call me.'

'Oh,' she considered, 'I hadn't thought of that. You're right. Well, sometimes John Horse called me Sharp in English.'

'Sharp?' I repeated. 'Because you carry around that big knife, or because your tongue is occasionally a lethal weapon.'

'Both,' her brother answered for her.

'And you,' I said, turning to the boy. 'I apologize for calling you Little Cloud. You got a snappier moniker?'

'I don't know what those words mean,' he confessed, 'but sometimes she calls me Duck because I like to swim.'

'No,' she corrected, 'I call him that because of the way he used to cry like a duck when he was a baby.'

The boy looked at me very seriously. 'I didn't cry.'

I nodded. 'Sharp and Duck; I'm Foggy. And what an oddly named trio we are. All right?'

They both nodded back.

'Good,' I went on, picking up the pace again, 'now let's go figure out what the hell just happened, and see if we can't find your mother.'

A few minutes later we were sitting inside Yudda's, at the bar. Early morning light through the diner windows gave the place a romantic appearance, even though it was only the size of a railroad car. There were five booths, five tables, and five seats at the bar. Everything was wood that Yudda had salvaged a long time ago from God knows where. The smell inside was like you were in the middle of an old barbecue oven. The ceiling was only the underside of an ancient, rusted tin roof.

The owner was standing at the grill, a cup of his famous Brunswick stew in hand, instead of coffee.

'You kids hungry?' he asked.

'No matter what they say,' I butted in, 'they had no breakfast, so fix up something suitable, right?'

He winked. He was the sort of person who could pull it off. They're very rare, the sort that winks and doesn't look stupid.

'It's got to be shrimp and grits,' he said, his big back turned our way.

'What about the skate wing?' I asked.

'For breakfast?' he wanted to know, as if I were a dope.

'Why did we leave that building?' Sharp demanded again, only a little more gently. 'We were about to find our mother!'

'No,' I told her in no uncertain terms, 'we were about to get into lots and lots of trouble. There was some kind of deal going down over there, in that office. You have to realize that. I don't know what it was, but a crooked cop with a loaded gun in an abandoned building? That doesn't smell like trouble to you?'

'Brady,' Sharp muttered.

'You think Brady's crooked?' Yudda asked without turning around.

He'd loaded up the grill with unpeeled shrimp, probably about half an hour out of the sea. In the corner, there was a giant pot. He stirred it, smiled, tossed in half a stick of butter and stirred again – all of which meant *grits* to me.

'Well, see, Brady's over there in the old abandoned bakery

on Blake Road arguing with some guys,' I said, 'and when I
called him out, he got rid of me like I was bad news.'

'He don't like you,' Yudda said.

'I know, but there was more to it.'

Sharp turned to me, tugged on my sleeve, and got me to
look in her eyes.

'OK. Foggy. We have to talk.' She was ice cold.

'Go ahead.' I swiveled my bar stool, turned to face her.

'In private,' she said.

'This is as private as it's going to get. Yudda is a designated
witness in this matter. I appointed him last night. When
you're dealing with Child Protective Services, it's always a
good idea to have someone else, a third party, to confirm
what's happened between the case worker, which is me, and
the alleged child, which is you.'

Her eyes narrowed, and I could hear the wheels turning
in her head. She took a deep breath. 'John Horse sent me
and my brother into town on purpose – because we're unusual.
We're the only ones in the Panther clan with our unique . . .
abilities. Duck can track. And I can kill.'

I didn't blink. 'Go on.'

'My mother disappeared along with two other Seminole
women who worked at the Benton,' Sharp said, staring at
the countertop of the bar. 'Inquiries were made, to no avail.
We've been sent to find these women and bring them back
home. Any way we can.'

I shook my head. 'John Horse would not send two children
on any sort of mission like that. I know his reputation—'

'Duck and I have unusual abilities,' she repeated. 'That's
why John Horse hires us.'

'Hires you?' That's all I could think of to say.

'We get paid to do . . . to do all kinds of work for him.
This is just one thing.'

I took a deep breath. 'Let me get right about this. You've
both been sent to investigate the disappearance of Seminole
women, including your mother, from the Benton Inn, a
high-voltage establishment for rich swells?'

She glared. 'That's about the size of it.'

I shook my head and whirled my barstool. 'Then I've been

going about this all wrong. It's not a child abandonment case or a missing persons case. You stay here, eat something good, and let me have a gander over at the Benton.'

'You think you'll find something that we didn't?' Sharp asked me, obviously irate. 'What, exactly, are you looking for in the only place where we know my mother is *not*?'

'One woman missing from a place like that is difficult business,' I told her, heading for the door. 'More than that? It's an industry. I'm afraid I know what happened to your mother.'

The door shut softly behind me. I could hear Sharp talking, but she was speaking in the Seminole language and too fast for me to understand it.

FIVE

The Benton always reminded me of the Waldorf in the old days. You know: elegant, olde world ambience, snappy service, an air of quiet dignity. All of which I did my best to destroy in the first few seconds I was there, based on my aforementioned bias for bold action versus quiet charm.

As soon as I hit the lobby I announced, very loudly, 'I'm looking for a Seminole woman named Echu Matta; she's wanted in connection with a child abandonment case I'm working on with State and Federal government.'

The place was still as a tomb for a second, and then a tall man in a dark suit came racing my way, scowling like he was about to rain all over Pittsburgh.

'Sir, I am entirely at your disposal,' he said with a combination of ire and servitude that must have taken years to hone. 'May I escort you to our office?'

His hair was thinning on top, and slightly grey at the temples. He was underweight by about twenty pounds, and his hands were the cleanest set of mitts I'd ever seen, down to the clear varnish on his manicure. He wore a silver name badge that said *Robert.*

We moved closer to the front desk.

'Listen, Robert,' I told him very politely, 'I'll close down your little playhouse and you won't *believe* the amount of noise I'll make if you don't tell me who you're working with.'

'I don't know what you're talking about.' His face was a perfect blank.

Before I knew what hit me, Sharp came from behind, knife in hand. She leapt up on the desk to menace Robert eye to eye.

'He asked you who you're working with,' Sharp hissed, 'to kidnap Seminole women!'

'I'm calling the police,' Robert said, quite alarmed.

I hauled out my badge. 'Tell them I'm here.'

That stopped him. Flash a badge, any badge, and the hoi polloi will generally give pause.

'Let's see if we can't sort all this out in an orderly fashion,' I continued. 'Sharp? Please put your knife away. Robert? Tell me when you last saw Echu Matta.'

'I–I have no idea who that is,' he stammered.

Sharp did not put her knife away. She put it very close to Robert's nose. 'Martha,' she said to Robert.

'Oh, Martha,' he repeated, 'the, um, that woman.'

'Martha?' I asked Sharp.

'Mother told me,' Sharp snapped in my direction, 'that this moron couldn't pronounce her name, and all he could get was a perversion of Matta. So.'

'What – really – what,' was all that Robert could manage.

'You've had several Seminole women working here,' I said, 'and they've all disappeared recently. You didn't think someone would find that interesting?'

'Those women?' Robert asked in spite of himself. 'They were *Indians*?'

I couldn't help laughing just a little. 'What?'

He looked worried. 'I thought they were . . . I mean, they were very . . . dark-skinned. You know. Black. We were told that they quit. They weren't happy with their treatment here, though I can't imagine why. There was even talk of . . . of a lawsuit.'

I shook my head. '*They* told you they were filing a lawsuit.'

Robert frowned and looked away. 'Well, no. We . . . we were told.'

'By whom?' I asked.

Robert looked very nervous indeed.

'It was the . . . we have an off-duty policeman who works night security for us, you know, after I've gone home, and those . . . those women are here. He told me they were going to sue the hotel for . . . for discrimination. So, naturally, I thought—'

'Brady,' Sharp cursed under her breath.

'Hm?' Robert asked distractedly.

'His name was Brady,' she growled at him, swishing her knife.

'No,' Robert said quickly. 'It was that nice Officer Watkins. He was so sweet to the women who worked here, you know, asking them about their commute and worrying about their families. He's the one who told us they were unhappy. And then they just didn't show up for work after that. What's all this about?'

'Aw, Christ,' I muttered.

'What?' Sharp asked me. 'Watkins is the other policeman who was with us last night, right? What does this mean?'

'I'm afraid it means I was an idiot for a minute,' I confessed, heading for the door. 'But I'm better now.'

'What?' Sharp asked.

'Let's pick up your brother and go to the police station.' I sighed, and headed out the door.

SIX

The Fry's Bay police station was something out of the *Dragnet* TV show: all exposition and no nuance. Nothing on the walls but sick-beige paint. Nothing on the floor but linoleum made of scuff marks. Three desks, broken blinds, fluorescent lighting. Brady and Watkins were there. One other guy, new to the office. The whole place smelled like burnt coffee and bus station cigarettes.

I motored in, sat right down at Brady's desk. The kids flanked me.

Brady grinned. It was awful.

'Glad you're here, pal,' he said. 'We just got the trace from that plate, the one this kid gave us last night. It's got a punch-line. Want to hear it?'

I glared.

'Brooklyn plate.' He shook his head and his ugly grin got bigger. 'Car belongs to one Sammy "Icepick" Franks. Sound familiar?'

And just like that, it was 1965 and I was standing in Washington Cemetery, the old place at 5400 Bay Parkway. All my relatives were buried there; it had been a nice Jewish cemetery since the mid-1800s.

I was standing there with Pan Pan Washington, my best Brooklyn pal. I had just boosted a prime black Lincoln town car in flawless condition and Pan Pan was working on it. The cemetery was a fine and private place to alter a boosted chariot, and the work was proceeding nicely, when all of a sudden there was Icepick Franks, a genuine urban miscreant.

'I always wanted a ride like that,' he said.

It surprised us both, me and Pan Pan, and Pan Pan came around with a .44 in his hand, open for business.

Icepick was a cucumber. Just smiled.

'I meant I would buy it from you,' Icepick said.

Pan Pan didn't move.

'You are Sammy Franks, are you not?' I asked him in my most elegant manner.

I always thought it was a good idea, when I was that age, to insert a dash of elegance into everything.

'I am,' he confirmed, 'and thank you for not using my street moniker, an appellation which I abhor.'

It turned out that Icepick appreciated a dash of refinement as much as I did.

'Make us an offer,' Pan Pan said, all business.

'Five thousand,' Sammy snapped back.

'Dollars?' Pan Pan squawked before he could think better of it. He'd been hoping for five hundred.

'You are fiddling with the VIN, are you not?' asked Sammy.

Pan Pan shrugged.

'And you can produce a bogus title that will stand up under scrutiny, as well as just enough alteration to the ride so as to make it less recognizable to the previous owner,' Sammy went on. 'I know your work. You and Moscowitz are famous all over the borough for your acumen.'

'Be that as it may,' Pan Pan said, 'and I realize that I'm shooting myself in the foot here, but five thousand dollars is a lot of cabbage.'

'Oh. Well. A story goes with it.'

I was wise. 'You would like this to be a forgotten transaction.'

'I would.' He smiled. 'No talk around the neighborhood about it, or me – or my business.'

It was Sammy's business that was the primary concern. He was called Icepick because that implement was his chosen method of carrying out his business, which was putting people on ice. One smooth shove right at the base of the medulla oblongata, and there you were: dead.

'If you truly know our work,' I told him, 'then you know that we have a very strict policy of amnesia: we never remember *anybody* we do business with.'

'I believe you,' he said. 'My offer stands. I like this car.'

And when you thought about it, the Lincoln town car was perfect for his work: elegant enough to say *I have money, leave me alone*; a trunk big enough to accommodate his victims, and it looked a little like a hearse.

'I'll be finished in forty minutes,' Pan Pan said, returning his .44 to its holster. 'My associate Mr Moscowitz will handle the paper.'

And I did.

So, I knew exactly what car Brady was talking about, but my bond, both economically and morally, forbade me to admit it.

'Brooklyn plate,' I said. 'That's something. What's the guy's name, again?'

'They call the guy Icepick, for Christ's sake,' Brady complained. 'Knowing your history as I do, I believe you ran in the same circles up there in New York.'

I looked him right in the eye. 'Doesn't ring a bell.'

He glared back. 'Doesn't ring a bell.'

I shook my head. But my mind was running a hundred miles an hour. Why in hell would Icepick choose my little corner of obscurity in which to dump a dead body? Seemed like he'd done it on purpose. Was it a message?

I didn't want it to distract me from the kids and their missing mother, but it was certainly not helping my concentration. So.

'Look,' I told Brady, 'we're here because these kids have a mother.'

Brady stared.

'The mother's missing,' I went on. 'And she scrawled a message to them in the vacant building where they were staying last night. Where you found them.'

'What does it have to do with the dead body in the bay?' he asked, loudly.

'Nothing.' I leaned forward. 'I'm telling you that you have a problem here in town. Three Seminole women are missing from the Benton Inn.'

Brady looked down. It was only for a second, but I saw his expression change. He fixed it right away, though.

'Maids?' he snapped, louder. 'So what?'

'So they've been kidnapped!' I said, matching his volume. 'Somebody's kidnapping women and shipping them out of town from that abandoned bakery. The one, PS, where I saw you half an hour ago. So, either you're investigating that crime, or something is rotten in the state of Denmark!'

'Demark?' He blinked. 'You think someone is shipping women to Denmark?'

'Look, Brady!' I stood up. 'If I find out you're involved in some sort of human trafficking, I'll have your badge, your house, and your money, while you spend the rest of your life in prison.'

I was making just enough of a scene to make the kids nervous and to attract Watkins. He came over and stood beside Brady.

'Come on, Foggy.' Watkins sighed. 'You know we got a hard job here. And you know we can't discuss an ongoing investigation.'

I smiled. 'So there *is* an investigation.'

Watkins rolled his head around. 'Yes. All right. There's an investigation. I've spoken with the night manager at the Benton.'

'That would be Robert,' I said, mostly so he'd know I was wise.

'You know, then, that I was actually helping those women,' Watkins went on. 'The hotel was stiffing them – underpaying, overworking. They didn't like it. They came to me to see what recourse they might have under the law. I gave them advice and talked with Robert.'

'Robert wouldn't really know much about what upper management does,' I said, 'but it was nice of you to come to the aid of . . . Look, the kids are scared half to death about their mother. Can you give us a little sunshine here or not?'

Taking my cue, God love them, the kids did their best to look pathetic.

'Look,' Brady growled, 'the *sunshine* we're giving away here is that I didn't incarcerate these two vagrants. But that could change real good if you don't get the hell out of my face!'

'I know you got a job to do, Foggy,' Watkins said sympathetically. 'Why don't you just take care of the kids and let us take care of the crimes?'

I shook my head. 'See, all this is connected. For example, the kids saw the car that dumped a dead body.'

Watkins rubbed his face with his hands. 'Yeah. Yeah.'

'My bet is that you know the owner of the car,' Brady said. 'And when we prove that, you're in jail.'

'For what?' I asked.

'Obstruction,' Brady shot back.

'What about our mother?' Duck asked, sticking to his sad-child shtick.

Watkins licked his lips and started three times before he said, 'The problem is, we think they just went . . . I'm sorry, kids, but your mom and the two other women went on a bender.'

Sharp looked up at me. 'What's a *bender*?'

'There was some missing money at the hotel,' Watkins went on, 'and three Seminole women were seen at the bus station. We think your mom's in Miami on a kind of vacation, see.'

'You think our mother stole money and went to Miami?' Sharp laughed.

'Could have been one of the other women who actually stole the money,' Watkins said.

'One of those women is a pregnant seventeen-year-old,' Sharp told Watkins, a little incredulously, 'and the other is almost a hundred.'

Duck's face grew dark. 'Is he saying my mother stole money?'

'And left town,' Brady snapped. 'She don't care about you. She stole; she went to Miami to get liquored up the way you people do, and makum whoopee.'

'Look! In spite of what you *goyishe* cop racists like to think,' I snapped, maybe a little too hot, 'the Seminole people just don't steal, and not one of them I ever met is a drunk. So why don't you keep that *bender* talk to yourself and your white-hood buddies!'

Brady rose out of his seat. 'I've had just about enough of your attitude, Jew-boy!'

Sharp, suddenly playing the part of the adult in the room, put herself in between me and Brady.

'What Foggy means to say,' she told Brady, 'is that he disagrees with your theory about what happened to our mother.'

'We really do have eyewitnesses who saw the women at the terminal, Foggy,' Watkins intervened. 'All three.'

'Check it yourself if you want to waste half an hour,'

Brady went on. 'Ask the night clerk. See where they went. See if it's not Miami!'

'Come on, Foggy,' Sharp said, taking my hand.

'Yeah, run along, *Foggy*,' Brady sang out. 'But don't leave home. As soon as we have something on you for the *real* crime here in town, I'll be wanting to talk to you a whole lot. You and your buddy, Icepick.'

I locked eyes with Brady.

'When I find out what's really going on here,' I said quietly, 'you're going to find out what some people use an icepick for. And I'm going to dance on your grave in red shoes.'

Brady grinned and turned to Watkins. 'Does that sound like the threat of bodily harm directed at an officer of the law?'

Watkins glared at me. 'Get out, Foggy. Go on, seriously. Go home. Cool off.'

Sharp was tugging on my hand; Duck was already headed for the door.

'Yeah, you just go to the bus station,' Brady repeated. 'See what the new night guy says!'

As I turned to leave, I finally realized what he was saying.

SEVEN

'Where're we going?' Sharp asked when she realized I wasn't headed home.

'Bus station,' I mumbled.

'But the mean man said that was a waste of time,' Duck told me.

'Yeah, he did.'

Sharp turned to her brother. 'He knows something. Look at his face.'

Duck looked up at me and then nodded. 'That's how I look when I know I'm on the right trail of something or other.'

Sharp nodded. 'You added up two and two and something came out wrong.'

'That doesn't make any sense,' Duck complained.

'It'll make sense in a minute,' I told him.

The bus terminal in Fry's Bay was a relatively dismal affair: cleaned once a year, smelled like a locker room, gave the word 'dingy' a bad name. Crushed cigarette butts all over the floor, pictures of exotic ports of call on the walls: Cleveland, Ohio, Hollywood, Florida, and one that just said Maine. No picture.

The day clerk was a seventy-year-old man with bad teeth and a funny eye. When the three of us came through the door, he jumped. He'd been asleep.

There was an older woman with a scarf on her head looking down at her hands; a teenaged poster boy for acne slumped down beside her. Otherwise, empty.

'Hello, Howard,' I said to the ticket guy.

'Mr Moscowitz?' he said like he wasn't sure it was me.

'You got a new night guy,' I told him. 'What's his name?'

'Melvin.'

'Where's Melvin now?'

'How would I know?' Howard shot back.

I reached in my pocket and fetched a fiver. Held it high.

He glanced at it and then blinked.

'Oh, Melvin. Yeah. He's at the Flamingo Motel. Room three.'
He reached for the five.

I pulled it back. 'Got a bus to Miami?'

'Every day.'

'What time?' I asked, handing him the bill.

'High noon,' he said, snatching the money out of my hand.

'No, I mean the night schedule,' I said.

'Ain't but one bus to Miami, Foggy. High noon.'

I looked down at the kids. 'There's not a night-time bus to Miami.'

'But . . .' Duck began.

'Flamingo,' Sharp interrupted.

I headed for the door. 'Room three.'

The Flamingo Motel was a genuine Florida relic. It had a giant neon flamingo, no longer in operation, and a vacancy sign that was always lit up. When the town was a haven for a certain type of nouveau riche clientele, the Flamingo had been a kitschy sort of hangout. The rumor was that Kerouac was staying there when he found out that *On the Road* was going to be published. The fact that everybody knew he'd been in Orlando when he heard didn't dissuade the local legend one bit. But it didn't really give the Flamingo's vacancy sign any relief either.

The whole place had probably once been pink, but time, salt air and neglect had turned it some color that didn't really have a name – unless *sorrow* was a color.

The number three on Melvin's door had swung sideways so it looked more like a W. It bounced a little when I knocked.

Melvin was not immediately in evidence.

'Officer Moscowitz!' I announced. 'Child Protective Services! Open up!'

That produced moaning, a bit of a shuffle and, at length, the face of Melvin in the doorway.

'What?' He was a runt with a crewcut in boxer shorts and a T-shirt that had the number seven on it.

I held out my badge. He flinched.

'Brady told me to speak with you,' I said, voice lowered. 'It's about three Seminole women who took a bus to Miami.'

Melvin looked around, eyed the kids, then stepped back. 'Come on in.'

We did.

The room was dark, with a blackout curtain. He snapped on the lamp beside the bed. Didn't help much. A bed with one bedside table, a chair with a missing arm, a dresser with no drawer pulls, and a little table that was supposed to be some sort of desk – all of it cracked and scuffed and generally ready for the scrap heap.

Melvin sat on the bed and lit a cigarette.

'Christ,' he said, and when he did the word was shrouded in smoke.

Sharp looked up at me. 'I don't understand what's going on.'

'The two and two I added wrong,' I told her, 'involved Watkins and Brady. I got them mixed up. Watkins looks like the good guy, but I think he's the crook.'

'And how,' Melvin managed weakly.

'But, he's so *mean*,' Duck said.

'Brady?' I nodded. 'Yeah. Chances are he's playing some kind of part. Don't know what yet. Or why. But he wanted us to come talk with Melvin here.'

'Watkins give me a hundred dollars to say them three women took a bus to Miami,' Melvin admitted. 'To say they's all liquored up.'

'But you didn't see them at the bus station?' Sharp asked.

Melvin shook his head.

'Kind of a stupid plan,' I began. 'All I had to do was ask Howard about the bus to Miami.'

Melvin shrugged. 'I'm supposed to say how Howard's a little addled, which he is. We have a local from Savannah on Thursday nights. That's when them three women got on. Being a local means it makes every stop between here and Miami, see, but it eventually gets there. Miami. Cheapest way to go.'

'Did Watkins give you any reason?' I asked.

'You know how he is,' Melvin said, taking another drag on his cigarette. 'Said he's trying to help them ladies.'

'Help them do what, exactly?' I asked.

'Said they's trying to get away from Brady,' Melvin

answered. And when he said Brady's name it sounded like he was cursing – a vulgar noise.

I shook my head.

Then, to my surprise, Sharp took my hand. 'Let's go back to your apartment,' she said softly.

'I have a few hundred more questions for Melvin,' I objected.

'Yeah,' she said, 'but you're not going to get any answers that matter. Trust me. Come on.'

Her face was convincing. I didn't know why, but it was.

'Melvin,' I said, 'what would it take to convince you to forget that we paid you a visit?'

'I'd like to forget everything about this town,' he said. 'Brady makes me nervous and Watkins is weird and now there's little Indian children in my room and I don't understand any of it.'

It was then that I noticed a distinctive aroma coming from his smoke. They were Kools all right, but he'd packed them half full of weed. Melvin wasn't sure which end was up.

I smiled, backing away. 'Yeah, kid. Probably better just to try to forget it all.'

He nodded, knocked the burning ash off the tip of his Kool, set the rest of it on the bedside table and fell back on the bed.

He was asleep before we were out the door.

And when I opened my apartment door I understood why Sharp had been so anxious to get me there.

'Hello, John Horse,' I said.

He was standing in the kitchen chopping up celery.

John Horse was more imaginary than real. He accomplished such a condition by never completely giving over to ordinary reality at all. Some people in his family told me he was over a hundred years old. Two told me that his body was dead but his spirit was unwilling to go along with it. What you'd call a Trickster, with a capital T.

None of that kept him from making a mess in my kitchen.

'Come on in, Foggy,' he told me. 'I'm making soup. I got a wild turkey this morning, and I thought the kids could use a nice home-cooked meal.'

'*Capoca-lakko!*' Duck called out.

It meant *big grandfather.*

'You sent these kids into town to find their missing mother all on their own,' I said to John Horse, headed toward the kitchen.

He looked up, surprised. 'They're not all on their own. They're with you.'

'We told you he sent us,' Sharp reminded me. 'And we said he told us about you.'

'Yeah,' I protested, 'but that's not . . . Look, we have a complicated type of situation on our hands.'

'Oh,' John Horse said, resuming his kitchen work. 'You mean the dead body in the bay.'

How he knew that bit of the story, I couldn't have said. Although there was probably gossip about it already.

'And you realize that the kids' mother isn't the only woman missing,' I went on, trying to stay a few steps ahead of him.

'Twenty-seven in all,' he told me. His voice had gone quiet.

I blinked. Twenty-seven women. That had to be a third of the entire female population of John Horse's village. But I wanted to stay calm for the sake of the kids. So.

I turned to Sharp. 'You knew he was here, of course.'

'I was pretty sure.' She nodded.

'And now you've got me all in the middle of things,' I accused John Horse.

He shrugged. 'A missing woman isn't really your business – even a lot of missing women. And a dead body in the bay, I mean, that doesn't happen every day in Fry's Bay, but it still isn't something you'd ordinarily involve yourself in, right?'

'*Very* right.'

'So, I used the kids to tie the two things together,' he concluded, 'and *get* you involved.'

Like it was simple. Obvious.

'I have things to say to you,' I began, steaming a little, 'but a whole lot of them involve language I'd rather not use in front of the minors. So, let's start with the big one.'

'Why did I get you involved?' He glared at me like I'd insulted him. 'Jesus, Foggy, you're usually quicker than that. I got you into this mess because I don't like the police in this town but I do like you. Because I don't trust the police in this town but I trust you. You and I, we can accomplish things together that it would take a hundred ordinary people to do.'

'We needed your help,' Sharp interrupted.

I shook my head. 'No. If John Horse needs my help, he knows he could just ask me.'

'Yes, but I needed you to see the kids,' he told me. 'To be committed to them, at least a little, and to see Brady and Watkins for what they are. Before you found out who was the dead body in the bay.'

'What do you mean, "who was the dead body in the bay"?' I stared at him.

'I mean that once you find out, you'll be tempted to concentrate on that.' John Horse locked eyes with me. 'And I needed to have, you know, the bigger picture.'

'All right,' I said, more irritated by the second. 'I'll bite. Who's dead in the bay?'

'I'm sorry, Foggy,' he told me. 'It's your Brooklyn friend, Pan Pan Washington.'

EIGHT

In the early days, in Brooklyn, Pan Pan and I were inseparable. He could turn a Volkswagen into a Studebaker if he wanted to; he was that talented in his chosen art form, which was altering cars I boosted in the borough. It was a match made in heaven. We liked the same clothes, the same music, even the same girl a couple of times. The fact that I was a Jew and he was black didn't even enter the picture. We were related in a larger family.

Now, Pan Pan wasn't a member of my *organization*, see, because you had to be a Jew for that. So not everybody saw our friendship the way we did. There was a Brooklyn gang who called themselves Zulu Nation, even though none of the guys had ever even been to Harlem, let alone Africa. Still, they were very uncomfortable with the amount of time I spent hanging out with Pan Pan on their turf. And some of my guys – a sort of Hebrew mafia, which I don't like to discuss – did not care for the color of Pan Pan's skin. Which was a very nice caramel color, but that was really beside the point.

I used to say to Pan Pan, 'Look, it's 1970, for God's sake. This kind of racism and anti-Semitism, it's a thing of the past. Ignore it.'

So I ignored it when the Zulus poured gasoline on a Coupe de Ville I'd moved; lit it up like an Italian bonfire. And Pan Pan ignored it when two apprentice mugs from Murder, Inc. walked into his mother's kitchen and asked her which of Pan Pan's body parts she wanted to use to flavor her collard greens.

When I told my mentor, Red Levine, about that, he stood by me. The day after I told him, one of the *mugs* had to learn how to shoot a pistol with his thumb because his trigger finger was missing. The other guy just split altogether, went to Montana, of all places.

But Red couldn't do a thing about the Zulus. That situation was kind of coming to a head when I absconded from

Brooklyn under difficult circumstances. I may have mentioned that I popped a car that had a baby in the back, and when the mother saw the car driving away, she chased it and had a heart attack.

Which is why I split. There's more to the story, but I don't like to go on about it. I send money to the kid's adoptive parents every month, anonymously. And I work for Child Protective Services – a kind of never-ending Yom Kippur. I'm atoning.

So, not only was I in shock to hear that Pan Pan was dead, and upset about it; I also began to wonder if I'd had anything to do with his getting iced. I know it's a cliché, but for me guilt is bone marrow.

I stood in my kitchen, staring at John Horse for quite a while before he spoke again.

'You think you had something to do with his death,' he said softly, like he'd read my mind.

I nodded.

'I was afraid of that.' He sighed. 'I can see it on your face.'

I sat down at the kitchen table. 'You understand that if Icepick did the job, I have to go after Icepick.'

'Icepick is the name of the man whose car the kids identified?' he asked. 'That's a difficult name to live with.'

I turned to the kids. 'Tell me everything you saw that night. Come here.'

The kids glanced at John Horse and he nodded. They came and sat at the table with me.

'I heard the car,' Duck began. 'It was, like, prowling.'

'Explain,' I said.

'Like the driver was looking for something.'

'Seemed suspicious,' Sharp said. 'We followed it.'

'Just so I have it right,' I interrupted, 'you were in the abandoned building on Blake, heard a suspicious car, and followed it down to the docks.'

'I thought it might have something to do with our mother,' Duck said. 'It was a very odd car.'

'Yeah,' I said. 'I'm familiar with the car. Go on.'

'The driver got out,' Sharp continued, 'and when a stray dog started to bark, he shot it.'

'That made me mad,' Duck said, 'but she wouldn't let me yell at the guy.'

'Because the next thing he did was open up his trunk and haul out a dead body,' Sharp went on.

'Was it wrapped up in anything?' I asked. 'Or was it loose?'

She shook her head. 'It was wrapped in something – maybe a tarp, like painters use. And that was held together with tape.'

'So, you didn't actually see the body.' I looked over to John Horse. 'Now I have to ask you: what makes you think the stiff was Pan Pan?'

John Horse stopped his kitchen work again. 'Why is he called that? Why is that his name? I want to know.'

'He was fixing a car once,' I answered impatiently, 'and it started to leak oil on to his face, because I'd hit something when I boosted it, and he was yelling at me about the oil pan. "Pan! Pan!" I laughed. The moniker stuck. What makes you think he's the stiff?'

He sighed. 'When I tell you that I know things before they happen, you never believe me.'

'Because you're usually making it up!' I shot back.

'Sometimes I am and sometimes I'm not. This time I'm not. The coroner is eventually going to identify the body as Pan Pan Washington. I heard the name in my sleep. How would I hear that name, other than a message from the future?'

'God!' I smacked a hand on the table. 'You've heard me talk about the guy for two years!'

'Yes,' he admitted. 'But you never talked to me in my sleep.'

'You know you make me crazy.' I stared.

'I don't think anyone can *make* you crazy, Foggy. I think you're either crazy or you aren't. And you aren't. So, ask me the next question.'

'What?'

'You have more questions.'

'Well, yes,' I admitted. 'I do. A lot of them, actually.'

'Why would Icepick kill your friend in Brooklyn and then drive a million miles to Fry's Bay to dump the body?'

'Except to send me a message.'

'You take it personally,' he said. 'Good. I want you to.

Because let me tell you that his actions are somehow connected with our problem, our tribal problem.'

I didn't know where to begin. 'Tribal problem?' I said finally. 'It isn't just the women who went missing with the mother of these children,' he said. 'So far there are twenty-seven women stolen from our tribe. Our little tribe out there in the swamp. Still at war with the United States Government. Still illegal in our own land. Still waiting for the larger justice. And now, without women, you understand, we'll vanish. We'll be gone from history.'

It hadn't been a passionate speech. He was just stating the facts. But it evoked in me such a profound feeling, I could barely speak.

'I understand, John Horse. But how is it – how is that connected to the murder of my friend from Brooklyn?'

'I don't know,' he said. 'That's why I got you involved. You see that.'

I looked at the kids. They were expressionless, like the faces of a lot of the people in John Horse's little village. They weren't stoic, exactly. They just processed emotion in a different way.

And what I realized was that I had to help the kids. A) It was my job. B) I liked them. C) The aforementioned atonement. So.

'There are only a few things in life I trust,' I said to John Horse. 'Among them I count my aunt's cooking, my friendship with Pan Pan, and you. If you say these two things are connected, I believe you.'

'Good,' he said, returning to his kitchen duty.

We spent the rest of the day discussing.

NINE

I had a full house that night. John Horse slept on the floor, Sharp and Duck managed the sofa together. I had a restless night in my bed, waking up five or six times thinking about Pan Pan.

Six in the morning came earlier than usual, but while I was putting on my suit, I could smell coffee. John Horse was already up. He made great coffee: ground whole beans by hand and put them right into the boiling water. I don't know what else he added, but it was the best coffee I ever had. I finished tying my tie as quick as I could just so I could get a cup.

Duck and Sharp were sitting at the kitchen table eating scrambled eggs.

When I appeared, John Horse held out a mug in my direction.

'Already poured,' he said. 'It's strong.'

'Stronger the better,' I mumbled. 'Had a bad night.'

'You were thinking about your friend,' he said. 'That's why we're going to find out about that today.'

'I have a plan,' Duck said.

Made me smile. Kid the size of a radiator had a plan.

'I'm going over to the Benton,' he went on. 'Talk to the new maids they got over there. They might say things to a little kid that they wouldn't tell a white man with a badge.'

I nodded. 'I guess there would be new maids, since the old ones are gone.'

'Cuban girls,' John Horse said. 'Imported from the Benton's sister hotel in Tampa.'

I sat down at the kitchen table with the kids. 'How you know that is something I'll leave alone. But Duck's plan is a good one.'

'That's not all of it,' he said. 'While I'm there, my sister is going to poke around at the bakery.'

'That, I'm not so crazy about,' I said, gulping the coffee.
'Dangerous.'

She smiled. 'I have a big knife.'

'I should go with you,' I began.

'You're going to be with John Horse,' Duck said sharply.
'The two of you are dealing with the adults.'

'We're going to the police,' John Horse said. 'They'll
confirm that the dead body is your friend, and then they'll
ask you all sorts of questions, and I'll listen, and I'll be able
to tell what's what.'

I glared at the old guy. 'No idea what you're saying. You're
trying to get me to go along with your Seminole mystic
shtick, but I don't buy it.'

'Oh, you buy it,' he said, grinning. 'You just have buyer's
remorse after you do.'

'Ha,' I said humorlessly.

'Eggs?' he asked me.

Twenty minutes later we all left my apartment. Duck
was off to the Benton, Sharp to the abandoned buildings
on Blake Road, and John Horse and I ambled toward the
police station.

You don't really walk *to* someplace with John Horse.
He doesn't ever seem to have a destination in mind. He's
just walking. He stopped to pet a stray dog and talk to it in
Muskogee, one of the Seminole languages. He pushed the
button on the corner to make the light change, even though
we weren't crossing the street.

'Think how many hundreds or maybe thousands of people
have touched that button,' he said as we walked on. 'And now
I have. Now I have a part of all those people on my skin.
Now I understand the world just a little bit better. Not enough
to make a difference by itself, but these things add up.'

I shook my head. 'Stop it. I know you're doing this just
to make me, like, take you seriously.'

'Do you know where the name "Doubting Thomas" comes
from?' he asked me.

'No idea.'

'It's from the Christian religion. The apostle Thomas refused
to believe that Jesus had been resurrected until he could put

his hands directly on the body of his Messiah, touch the death wounds, feel the blood.'

'Look, I go this Thomas guy one better,' I told him. 'That guy's not *my* Messiah, no matter how many times I poke a finger in his side.'

He nodded. 'I always find that confusing, the difference between the Jews who do believe in Jesus and the ones who don't.'

'No, see, it's the Roman Empire that believed – the Jews didn't ever. Why are you talking about this? It's very irritating.'

He stopped walking. 'To distract you. We're at the police station. And you have to be a little irritated when you're talking with them this morning.'

I looked around and, sure enough, we were at the front door of the station. I decided to go with his theory of irritation, even though I didn't exactly know why.

I shoved through the door and started talking before I was barely into the room.

'Now look what you've made me do,' I announced. 'You've made me get up this early in the morning and come here with John Horse. I hope you're happy!'

Watkins was the only one in. He looked up at me like I'd thrown a dead puppy on his desk.

'Foggy?' He glared.

'The missing Seminole women did *not* go to Miami, as you well know,' I barreled on. 'And the dead body in the bay turns out to be a friend of mine. Did you know *that* when I was in here yesterday with the kids?'

He blinked three times really fast and then started sputtering. John Horse's strategy was working.

'The women did . . . Foggy, why would you . . . Listen.' He swallowed, gathering his thoughts. 'Brady's out to get you, you know that. He doesn't like you, and he hates those little Indian children. Once he knows that the dead body was a friend of yours, I don't know if I'll be able to keep him under control.'

'So, you *do* think that the deceased is someone I know,' I shot back.

He glanced down at his desk. 'Got the report here.'

'That was fast,' I said.

'How many dead bodies do you think the County Coroner has to look at in any given week?'

'Just a guess,' I said, 'but this one made it a busy week for him.'

'Right.' He opened the file folder. 'Albertus T. Washington, aka Pan Pan. For some reason. Cause of death was a pointed object inserted into the base of the skull. Pointed object like an icepick, maybe. And you knew the guy, this Pan Pan?'

All I could think about in that moment was the way Pan Pan laughed. You couldn't feel bad when you heard that sound. It made you biologically incapable of gloom.

'Yeah,' I said, looking down at the floor. 'I knew the guy.'

'Well.' Watkins closed the file. 'That's suspicious, don't you think?'

'Very,' I agreed.

'I'm very impressed by the efficiency of the Fry's Bay Police Department,' John Horse said. 'Cause of death, victim identification, and association with Mr Moscowitz, all in a little more than twenty-four hours. That's something.'

His voice wasn't edged with any kind of irony; he really did sound impressed. But I knew better. He was trying to point out to me what I already knew. The Fry's Bay Police Department wasn't capable of tying its own shoe in twenty-four hours, let alone conducting an investigation of that ilk in such an abbreviated timeframe.

'How *did* you find out the identity of the victim?' I asked, trying to match John Horse's disingenuous tone.

'From his driver's license,' Watkins said, a little tauntingly, like it should have been obvious to us. 'And his American Express card.'

Except that Sammy 'Icepick' Franks always removed ID from his victims. Always. Part of his professionalism. So, either the cops were lying, or Icepick had deliberately left Pan Pan's wallet on the body.

One way to find out.

'You don't have his driver's license,' I snapped, dialing up the irritable quotient.

Watkins squinted, popped open the file, and held up a Xeroxed page of Pan Pan's ID.

Which meant Icepick had deliberately left it on the body. Which gave me a stupid ray of hope.

'Any other tests or anything to identify the body?' I asked.

'What for?' Watkins growled. 'We got his *driver's license!*'

But I knew cops in Fry's Bay. Hence my ray of hope. Dead black guy plus bad Motor Vehicle Department photo – swear to God, the stiff could have been almost anybody. Any black face equaled any other black face.

'Can I see the body?' I asked.

'No!' Watkins had decided to match my tone of irritability. 'Only next of kin.'

'He was a friend of mine!' I said. 'I'd like to say goodbye.'

'Say goodbye at the funeral,' he sneered, closing the file. 'And if I were you, I'd get out of here before Brady comes in.'

'Fine!' I said. 'But I'm still looking into the thing about the kids' mother.'

'Foggy . . .' he began.

'It's my job, Watkins,' I said, turning away from him. 'That's what they pay me for: protecting the child, and every child needs a mother. So.'

I made a concerted effort to storm out. John Horse followed.

When we were out on the street he said, 'That went well.'

I smiled. 'I thought so.'

The abandoned bakery smelled like rust and dead birds. I called out for Sharp, but she wasn't there. John Horse took three steps into the building and began to shake his head.

'Something terrible happened here,' he muttered.

I said, 'What makes you say that?'

'Can't you feel it?'

I looked around. 'I feel cold.'

'It's . . .' he began, and them something caught his eye. 'Look.'

He pointed to something in a far corner. Looked like a couple of bird corpses. He headed in that direction; got there before I did.

There were feathers and bones and blood – desiccated guts of some sort.

'Bad.' John Horse stared.

I looked around. All over the floor there were bird feces. The pigeons or whatever they were had made a home in the rafters of the joint for years.

'A couple of birds died in the corner?' I asked him.

'Look closer, Foggy.'

I did. 'All right,' I said after a second. 'Some cat or small animal caught a couple of birds and ate them.'

He sighed. 'Look at the way the feathers are arranged.'

I tilted my head and tried to see what he saw. After a moment, I thought I understood, even though I didn't like it.

'That's not what I think it is,' I began.

He nodded. 'Someone ate the birds raw. And then that person tied together the feathers and bones in that exact pattern.'

'What is it?' I stared down at the thing.

'I believe someone was trying to imitate Stikini.'

'I don't know what that is,' I confessed.

'Evil owl beings. By day they look like Seminole people, but at night they vomit up their souls and their internal organs. They do that so that they can eat human hearts. All you have to do is speak their name and you might turn into one. So, don't say their name out loud. I can do it because I know how to ward them off. But you – just in case, don't say it, all right?'

'Right,' I confirmed. 'What the hell is going on with this?' I touched it with the tip of my Florsheim shoe.

'I'm not sure,' he answered, staring at it.

'I mean, these aren't owl bones or feathers,' I said. 'Even I know that.'

'No, but doesn't the desperation of eating a raw bird say something?'

'It says, "don't talk about it very much more or I'll lose my breakfast."'

He nodded. 'At least.'

'The thing is,' I began, looking around at the whole innards of the bakery, 'the kids' mother, and the other Seminole women, ended up here in a container. It was probably put on a truck and shipped out. We think their mother is a victim of human trafficking.'

He closed his eyes. 'I was afraid of that. And it makes this Stikini double trouble. One of two things. One of the women who's been kidnapped has become an owl demon; or the creatures who kidnapped them were owl demons.'

'Or,' I said, squinting, 'it could mean that the person who was so hungry she ate a raw bird was trying to tell us that these people who took her were wrong all the way to the ground.'

He looked at me. 'You mean she might have just been trying to convey the extreme nature of the kidnappers.'

'Or raw pigeon gave her some kind of god-awful food poisoning and she, like, hallucinated or something.'

'All good possibilities,' he said. 'But they all mean that the women are being mistreated on top of being taken against their will.'

'Starved, held here or somewhere else for days before being shipped out.'

'What could be worse?' He swallowed.

'I'll tell you what's worse,' I said. 'I think the cops are involved.'

'In the kidnapping?'

'Watkins and Brady gave me the runaround,' I told him. 'They also lied to me.'

'Officer Brady has been a problem for us for a while.'

'Yeah,' I hedged, 'that's just it: I actually think Watkins might be a bigger rat.'

'Really?' John Horse was quite surprised. 'He's always so courteous.'

'*One may smile and smile and be a villain,*' I told him.

'*Hamlet,*' he said right back. 'Act one, scene five.'

'Really?' I shook my head. 'I only ever heard Red Levine say it.'

'Your mentor. He was well-read, then.'

I nodded. 'I guess.'

He turned my way. 'You're wondering where Sharp is. You're worried about her.'

I nodded. 'She's an odd kid.'

'She can take care of herself, Foggy.'

I shook my head. 'If she can take care of herself, why did you send her to *me*? When she comes to me, I'm supposed to take care of her. That's the job.'

'I already told you: I thought if you met her, you'd want to help her find her mother before you tried to find out who killed your friend. It was completely selfish on my part.'

'And that's another thing,' I said. 'How did you know that Pan Pan was dead?'

'I told you that, too, didn't I?' he asked. 'I had a dream.'

Just as I was about to object to that statement, we heard a noise upstairs.

The open part of the bakery on the ground floor was all industrial ovens and shadows. The best light in the place came from high windows close to the ceiling. And up a rickety set of iron stairs were the offices, about a tenth of the footprint of the downstairs. That's where the noise had come from.

I headed right for the stairs. I thought that Brady was probably up there, maybe with other people, like before. John Horse caught up with me and touched my arm; shook his head.

'Who's there?' he called out in a voice that sounded like a sick, scared old man. Which John Horse was not, but it was a pretty good trick.

No response.

'Come down here,' he called out again.

Nothing.

'I'm going up,' I told him and took the first step before he could stop me.

'Foggy,' he began.

But I was already bounding up the stairs. I wanted to confront Brady, ask him a few questions. Maybe punch him a few times, to make myself feel a little better.

Top of the stairs, still no sound from anything or anyone. I peered into the offices, all glass fronted, all in spectacular disarray.

I moved toward one of the three doors, and heard the noise

again. I twisted my head around the doorway in the direction of the sound.

Crumpled on the floor next to one of the steel desks was a nearly lifeless body. It took me a second to realize who it was. The big knife in her little hand was the clue.

TEN

For various reasons, I was known at the Fry's Bay Hospital. Maggie Redhawk was the head nurse, and a friend of mine. She tried for the third time to explain the difference between the words *unconscious* and *coma*. 'A coma is like the worst kind of unconsciousness,' she said. 'But it's on the same spectrum, see? Being unconscious is like a deep sleep. Being in a coma is more like *dead*, except for biological functions. Did the kid have anything to drink or is she on any kind of drugs?'

That last question was directed at John Horse. It was an offensive question, but Maggie was right to ask. Young Seminole people around Fry's Bay were very interested in cheap wine and good weed.

But John Horse shook his head. 'This is Topalargee.'

Maggie's face changed. 'Oh.'

I'd never seen Maggie silenced by anything, but the mention of the kid's name stopped her in her tracks. She just stared.

After a moment, John Horse continued. 'Who's the best doctor in this place?'

'Whit–Whitlock,' she stammered. 'Right.'

And she was gone.

'The kid's got a rep in your community, I see,' I said.

'She was born dead,' he told me. 'And then she wasn't dead. Do you have any idea what that means?'

'Medically speaking, a little. Spiritually speaking, I think you're about to tell me.'

'Her body was born,' he said right away, 'while her spirit was still in the other world. She spent extra time in Great Beyond before she came into her body. She has extra knowledge, an understanding of things that you and I can't understand. That's partly what she's doing now, being unconscious. She's communing in the other world. When she's learned whatever it is that she needs to know, she'll come back to us.'

'Do you actually believe that,' I asked him, 'or is that part of your performance as the "wise old Seminole"?'

He looked over at the kid. '*She* believes it. That's what counts.'

I shook my head. Not because I didn't believe what he was saying, exactly. More because I didn't want to buy into his line. I admired the guy, but that didn't keep me from being skeptical of everything about him.

'Well, my only concern at the moment is finding whoever did this to her,' I said, staring at the little kid's bruised and bloody face, 'and explaining to them why it was a bad thing.'

A second later Maggie was back in, and a doctor out of some television show appeared in the doorway. Grey at the temples, spotless white lab coat, stethoscope around his neck, and a look of deep concern on his face.

'This is Doctor Whitlock,' Maggie explained unnecessarily.

'Who did this?' he asked, staring compassionately at the kid.

'I'll find out and get back to you,' I answered grimly.

He turned my way. 'You're Mr Moscowitz, from Child Protective Services.'

I nodded once.

'And you,' he went on, sizing up John Horse, 'are next of kin, I assume.'

John Horse smiled. 'Naturally you would assume that.'

'This is John Horse,' Maggie said instantly.

The doctor took a small step backward. 'Mr Horse,' he said foolishly.

'The girl is a unique element of our village in the swamp,' John Horse said.

He thought that would explain something or other, but the doctor didn't understand.

He just blinked and asked, 'How long has she been unconscious?'

'Can't be more than an hour or so,' I answered. 'We found her like this in the abandoned bakery at the end of Blake Road.'

'What was she doing there?' he asked, moving toward the bed.

'Investigating the disappearance of her mother,' I told him.

The doctor didn't hesitate; he reached for his scope and put it on her chest. But he said, 'Where is her mother?'

'Missing,' John Horse said before I could.

'Do you know what happened to this child?' he asked.

'Looks to me like someone beat her up,' I said.

'We checked for broken bones before we brought her here,' John Horse said at the same time.

'You shouldn't have moved her.'

'You think it was better to leave her lying in a pile of bird crap in an abandoned building?' I asked.

'Her pulse is weak,' he mumbled, ignoring me.

'Foggy,' Maggie said softly, 'why don't you take off? There's nothing you can do here.'

I nodded.

'I'll go too,' John Horse announced. 'We'll check back in.'

The doctor didn't even turn around.

John Horse and I didn't speak again until we were outside the hospital.

'I'm not complaining,' he said as we turned on to the sidewalk. 'But why is Topalargee still alive?'

'I get it,' I agreed. 'Why beat the kid up and then leave her there? Unless she was able to fight off her assailants and she only collapsed after they took off.'

'She still had her knife in her hand,' he agreed.

'Takes a certain kind of person to beat up a little kid,' I mused.

'Brady wouldn't mind it,' he said.

'I'm still trying to figure all that out,' I said. 'Brady, Watkins, the manager over at the Benton. Who's a bad guy and who's just stupid.'

'Why can't they be both? Where're we going now?'

'Benton,' I said, 'make sure Duck's OK.'

The guy at the front desk was someone I'd never seen before. He eyed John Horse up and down.

'Where's Robert?' I asked.

'He's not here,' the guy said impatiently. 'How may I help you?'

I flashed my badge so fast he flinched. 'Child Protective Services! How do you feel about obstructing a law enforcement officer in the operation of his duty?'

'Child . . . child . . .' He couldn't seem to say anything more.

'I'm looking for a Seminole kid of about eight or maybe nine,' I went on. 'He came over here asking about his mother.'

'He did?' The guy didn't have a clue.

'Maybe he went directly to the maids,' John Horse suggested.

'How would they help?' I asked. 'If they're Cubans, imported from Miami, they wouldn't know anything about this.'

'They might know who told them they were coming to Fry's Bay.'

I glared at the clerk. His name badge said *Tim.*

'So, Tim.' I leaned forward and put my badge away. 'How long have you worked here at the Benton?'

'Three years.' He swallowed.

'Did you know any of the service staff? The maids?'

'Those Negro women?' he asked.

'They were Seminoles.' I sighed.

'They *were*?' He shook his head. 'I don't think so.'

'Did you ever speak to them?'

'In passing,' he said, unable to fathom why it would matter.

'Any idea what happened to them? Why they aren't working here now?'

'They quit,' he said. 'Objected to the pay.'

'They told you this?'

'They were trying to negotiate higher wages with the help of an off-duty cop, a friend of theirs, apparently.'

I turned to John Horse. 'Watkins.'

'Interesting,' he said.

'What's this got to do with children?'

John Horse tugged on my arm. 'Come on, Foggy. He doesn't know anything.'

I looked at Tim's face. Truer words had never been spoken: Tim really didn't know *anything.*

'Where are the maids now?' I asked.

'I . . . Third floor, I think.' He squinted. 'I really don't think you should bother them while they're working. They'll be finished—'

'Tim,' I interrupted, 'if you say one more word, I'm going to have to charge you.'

'Charge me?' He glared. 'With *what*?'

He was right to ask. I had nothing. But when you've been hassled by the cops as much as I have, you knew the right words to say.

'Obstruction and resisting to start with,' I snapped. 'And I'll think of a couple more things before we get to the police station. Come on.'

I moved like I was coming around the desk to get him.

'OK, OK,' he said, holding up both hands. 'Third floor. Fine.'

But half an hour with the Cubans and another forty-five minutes looking around the hotel produced no new information and no Duck.

'I don't care for the way this is unfolding,' I told John Horse as we walked out of the Benton. 'One kid's in an almost-coma, the other's vanished altogether.'

He nodded. 'I should have told you something to begin with.'

The sunshine wasn't especially warm, or cheerful. But the street was bright, and the sky was cloudless. All I had to do was appreciate that until John Horse felt like going on. I was well acquainted with his penchant for the long pause. He'd used it on me in the earlier days of our relationship to get me to talk. See, a big silence in the conversation was a void that most people wanted to fill. But if you just relaxed and let the silence be silence, you could beat the old guy at his own game.

As we rounded a corner headed toward the donut shop, he said, 'I'm afraid that some of our own people are responsible for the missing women.'

I waited.

But that was all he was going to say.

I stayed quiet until we were sitting at the counter and the new girl – Bibi from Indiana, three weeks on the job – gave us each a cruller and a cup of mud.

When I couldn't take it any more, I said, 'You mean someone in the Seminole nation took the kids' mother?'

He nodded. 'But not someone from our little town out in the swamp. Businessmen.'

The way he said *businessmen* made me feel sick; the sound of it was so vile.

He was talking about Seminole men who had betrayed their heritage by selling oil rights to Exxon, cutting their hair and wearing Brooks Brothers suits. I could commiserate. I'd watched a lot of Jews in my neighborhood do just about anything they could to look like the goyim. No Star of David, open on Saturday, shortening the name from Moscowitz to Moss.

'Yeah,' I said, bite of cruller in my mouth. 'I wish you'd told me that right off, but I don't see what it would have done to affect the current situation.'

He shrugged.

Bibi wandered back over. Her face was a little red and she wouldn't look either one of us in the eye.

'Sorry,' she began. 'Sorry. Could you . . . would you mind paying for the donuts now?'

I glanced up at her.

'Problem?' I asked.

Her eyes darted left for a split second. 'No. Um.'

One of Fry's Bay's newer citizens was seated near the cash register, scrupulously avoiding my glare.

'That's Hackney, from Tampa,' I said to Bibi. 'He's the new proprietor at the hardware store. He just gave you some bad advice.'

'Foggy,' John Horse warned. 'Just pay for the donuts and let's go.'

I got up like I hadn't heard him, and went to sit down next to Mr Hackney. He was a pale, skinny goofus, five-foot-five, balding pate and lips as thin as dental floss.

'You just told our girl, Bibi, to get our cash up front, right?'

He turned to me defiantly. 'I've had ten or twelve of these coloreds in my shop since I got here – shoplifters and drunks. I was nice the first couple of times. Extended credit to a boy who said he was repairing the roof on his house and was about to go to work on a road crew. Ain't seen a whisper of him since. I just told the girl if she don't want the same kind of trouble, get the money now.'

I nodded. 'You're new in town, so I'm going to give you a friendly lesson in civics. First, this entire area is owned – *all* the land – by the Seminole tribes of Florida. You're only here because they agree to it. Second, you have a different concept of Time with a capital T than some other people. What I mean is, have a little patience: the kid who borrowed the roofing supplies will be back in eventually, and he'll probably bring you a little present along with the money. So, relax, OK? And if you haven't already paid for your donut, it's on me.'

I waved Bibi over before he could say anything.

'What's the damage for all three of us, Mr Hackney included?'

'Oh. Um.' Then she smiled at me. It was a face that could melt stone. 'Mr Hackney owes a dollar and a quarter. Yours is on the house.'

Hackney sputtered. I handed Bibi a fiver.

'Keep it, kid,' I told her. 'And despite the difference in our ages, I'm a little in love with you.'

She blushed, which only exacerbated my ardor.

John Horse had already finished his donut and coffee and was standing. 'Come on.'

But I had a weird hunch.

'Bibi,' I said, 'you know Officer Brady, one of our fine policemen here in town.'

She nodded.

'Was he in here night before last, by any chance? I know he usually comes in here, like, every night.'

She thought for a second. 'He was. Him and that nice Mr Watkins both. Late. But they got a call on the car phone and took off. Something about . . . it was about that body in the bay.'

'Were they alone, or was there anyone with them?' I asked.

'There was another man,' she said. 'Rich man, nice suit. He come in here a couple minutes after the cops. Nice car. Cadillac, I think.'

'You'd never seen him before?'

She shook her head and glanced in the direction of John Horse. 'But he was, you know, one of them.'

'He was a Seminole.' I did my best not to sound surprised.

She lowered her voice. 'Well, he was colored. But I think he was a Negro. Is there a difference?'

I didn't want to go into the whole rigmarole with her, but there were black Seminoles, descendants of freed or escaped slaves. They made it to the Florida swamps and married into the tribes there. They mostly lived apart, in separate bands. But since there'd been so much intermarriage, the lines were blurred. And when you factored the general observations of the hoi polloi – i.e. one colored face was more or less like any other – you dealt with a weird mix of racism and ignorance on a nearly constant basis. So, while I didn't blame Bibi for her comment, and I still had feelings for her, my ardor was somewhat abated by her lack of enlightenment.

'Did they say his name?' John Horse asked.

'The cops?' She shook her head. 'Nuh-uh. But they treated him like he was the boss. You know, called him *sir* and stuff.'

Hackney finally got himself together enough to say, 'I can pay for my own damn donut!'

All three of us stared at him.

'It's already covered,' Bibi said harshly, and made a big show of putting my fiver in the cash register near his elbow.

John Horse was already out the door.

ELEVEN

We were halfway down the block before John Horse spoke up.

'What made you ask that girl if there had been someone else with the cops that night?' he wanted to know.

I slowed my pace. 'Not sure, but I started to figure it this way. The cops are involved in some kind of human trafficking scam. Watkins was nice to the women at the Benton, but their natural Seminole suspicion of the cops would have prevented them from being convinced to come away with *him*. And you said there were Seminoles involved. So, I started thinking that maybe someone they *would* trust might have lured them away from the hotel.'

'You don't think the cops could have just taken them into custody or something? Or worse: drugged them?'

'My impression is that the mother of those children,' I answered, 'isn't someone who'd go gently. She would have kicked up a fuss.'

He nodded again and stopped walking. We were on the corner of a street that led down to the beach. He looked toward the ocean.

'Can you smell the salt?' he asked.

'Yeah, I smell tacos,' I went on, 'but my point is that neither of the managers at the Benton mentioned any kind of brouhaha. They both said that the reason the women left was on account of their wages.'

'All right, someone who was *not* Watkins persuaded them that they might get better pay,' he said thoughtfully. 'If he was a Seminole he'd have to be from the Oklahoma bands – the women would have known all the wealthy-looking Seminole men around here. And Watkins was just facilitating. So they thought. Is that about what you're thinking?'

'It is.'

He closed his eyes. 'That might explain the mess of feathers and bones we found in the bakery. Echu Matta made it to send a message, and Topalargee found it, or Topalargee made it herself before she passed out, to tell me something.'

'Right. There's a demon abroad in the land.'

He turned his gaze on me. 'You realize that sometimes your diction is ridiculous.'

I shook my head. 'It's *colorful*.'

'All right.' He sighed. 'I'm going back to the hospital so that when the kid wakes up, I'll be there. She can tell me what happened, without the colorful language. What are you going to do?'

'I think I might try to find out more about a visitor from Oklahoma.'

The Oklahoma Seminoles were all descendants of the more than three thousand Seminoles forcibly removed from Florida by the United States Government.

And, as I may have mentioned, they never signed a peace treaty.

While I had a beef with the crooked cops in Brooklyn, my feelings were nothing compared to the rage John Horse felt for the American government. And, frankly, you could see why. After the tribes were separated, they developed independently of each other, significantly confusing their cultural heritage. And to make matters worse, whenever the government could do it, they would ship young men away from Florida to Oklahoma under the guise of education: 'Better schools in Oklahoma.' And once they were gone, the kids never came back.

The idea that an Oklahoma Seminole had something to do with the disappearance of the kids' mother didn't sit very well with John Horse, because he would have figured that it somehow involved the US government. And he was probably right. He usually was.

It was about that point, as I stood there on the street corner smelling the salt air, that I realized I was beginning to think like John Horse. An alarming prospect.

He was nodding at me like he read my mind.

'All right, then,' he said. And without anything further, he turned in the direction of the hospital and headed off.

Myself, I thought it was about time for a lobster taco.

* * *

Yudda was the Einstein of culinary invention, always trying something new. For example – now this is in the exact middle of Nowhere, Florida, remember – he had recently devised a taco in which there was fresh-caught lobster, homemade slaw, home-grown peppers and some kind of sauce that was handed down to Moses from the mountain top.

The second I walked in the door, he read my face.

Without a word, he started working. 'Three?'

'Yes.' I sat in the last booth. Yudda mixed up the corn flour. It was going to take a minute to complete the creation, but great art takes time.

'Shot of tequila?' he offered.

'It's, like, eleven o'clock in the morning, man.'

He looked around for a second. 'Oh. Coffee, then?'

He poured without my answering.

'Hey, Yudda,' I said after the first sip, watching him flatten the taco flour, 'you're always prowling around at night.'

'I don't prowl,' he interrupted. 'I *gambol*. I frolic.'

'Have it your way,' I said. 'You're out and about after midnight.'

He nodded. 'I am.'

'In recent such sojourns,' I went on, 'you haven't seen, maybe, a Seminole swell, stranger, hanging out at the Benton, or with the cops at the donut shop?'

'I have.' He rolled his taco through the flattening part of a pasta maker, and it came out all funny shaped. But he scooped up a paring knife and made it a perfect circle in one smooth move. Then he scooped it up and slapped it on to the griddle. It puffed up instantly. Then he sang, very softly, 'Third-rate romance, low-rent rendezvous.'

After which he flipped the taco.

'What the hell are you singing?' I asked him.

'I heard it on the radio and now it's stuck in my head,' he complained. 'That ever happen to you?'

'Happens to everybody,' I said. 'It's the *job* of the pop song to stick itself in your ear.'

'I guess.' He took the first taco off and put the second one on.

'Are you going to tell me about the Seminole rich guy, or not?' I pressed.

'Oh, yeah. Big man. Over six foot. Nice suit. Seen him sitting with Brady and Watkins in the donut shop – oh, about once a month.'

'You mean you've seen him before this – he's been here more than just once recently?'

'That's right.'

Second taco dough golden, third one on the griddle.

'You saw him *just* at the donut shop?' I pressed.

He sighed and flipped the third taco.

'Would you let me concentrate on your dining experience?' he complained. '*After* I assemble your tacos, I'll give you my notes on the subject.'

'You took notes?' I asked.

'I took notes.'

There it was: Yudda's paranoia at work for me.

Yudda was convinced that a certain woman in New Orleans, whence he hailed, was after him. Sending investigators and paying off officials. I'd never gotten the full story out of him, but there was something about big money, small crimes and a secret identity. I'd even been told, by other denizens of Fry's Bay, that Yudda had once been in the CIA. That I didn't believe. He was too flamboyant – too *Cajun*.

But this paranoia occasionally resulted in valuable information. He'd seen dozens of crimes, several assaults and one entire notebook's worth of spouses cheating on spouses. A particular beef of his.

None of which he reported to the cops. But if he was in the right mood, and a little drunk, he'd share with me.

So, moments later, while I had a mouth full of lobster taco, he recited a page of Seminole sightings.

He concluded with, 'And finally, the donut shop night before last, when you asked me to come witness what happened with you and the kids and the cops.'

He looked up.

'You didn't think to mention this to me?' I asked.

He set his notebook down on the bar. 'Look. I know that

half of what I write down here is goofy. I know I'm paranoid. But I believe the old saying.'

'Just because you're paranoid doesn't mean they're *not* after you.'

'That saying,' he agreed. 'But I don't share my troubles unless somebody asks. You asked. I'm telling you.'

My conclusion, from the list of times and places this mysterious Seminole rich guy appeared in Fry's Bay, was that he did indeed have something to do with the missing women. My logic worked this way: if he was present on the night that Icepick dumped Pan Pan in the bay, he was no good.

Yes, it was a personal conclusion with absolutely no real logic, but you had to figure the guy was wrong just for hanging out with Watkins and Brady. And the timing of his visits to our little paradise was suspicious, because before the donut shop, Yudda had seen the guy at the Benton on what may have been the last night the kids' mother was there.

And I was also persuaded by John Horse's thinking that a Seminole man in a nice suit could convince Seminole women to come away with him much more quickly than a crooked cop could.

So, if the guy had been to the Benton, I thought it was best to go scare that kid, Tim, a little bit more. See if I could get him to tell me something about our mystery man.

Tim was not happy to see me. The second I walked in the door, he started talking.

'Look, *sir*,' he said without the slightest tone of respect, 'the police have told me that you're not a law enforcement official, so I don't have to answer any questions you ask me.'

Well. Two things: he was defensive, and the cops had been there in the short time since the last time I had.

'You've been misled,' I told him, motoring up to the front desk. 'I am an employee of the government and I am empowered to detain, arrest and incarcerate anyone I think might be endangering the life or wellbeing of a child. And currently I have my sights set on you. I have two kids under my protection whose wellbeing is seriously hindered by your attitude. So, step out from behind that desk, turn around and put your hands behind your back!'

Idle chatter on my part. I didn't have any handcuffs.

'Christ!' Tim yelped. 'What is it you people want from me? I'm just trying to save up enough money to pay for my next semester at FSU!'

'Oh,' I said, my tone completely changed. 'That can be a good school, I hear. What are you studying?'

He blinked. 'Hospitality management.'

'Oh, so this gig here at the Benton is kind of like a training program.'

'Work-study internship, yes.' He swallowed, and then lowered his voice. 'But this place is weird.'

'In what way?'

'In what way?' He glared. 'In the seven weeks since I've been here, the cleaning staff has turned over three times, the cops are in and out of here like it's a second home, and you keep scaring the bejesus out of me!'

'Well, maybe you had too much bejesus in you to begin with, so I'm doing you a favor, but I digress. All I really want to know is if you've seen a big guy, a well-dressed Seminole man, in this joint any time recently.'

'You mean Mr Talmascy,' he said right away.

'I do?'

He nodded. 'Expensive suit, perfect hair and a watch that could pay for my entire education.'

'And he's been here enough so you'd know his name.'

'Well, one of my electives, Special Topics in Hospitality, taught us how to spot what they call a *whale*.'

'They teach you that in college?' I shook my head. 'That's a gambling term: high roller, big spender.'

He nodded. 'Means the same thing in hospitality. You want to identify those guys and anticipate.'

'Got it. And what needs did you anticipate as regards this Mr Talmascy?'

Tim frowned. 'Couldn't quite figure him out. At first, I was afraid he was interested in getting *close* to the maids, if you know what I mean. I really didn't want to have to try to entice one of those women to go to his room at night. They scared me too, those women. Plus, I didn't really like the idea of being a . . .'

'Pimp,' I suggested.

'Go-between,' he corrected instantly.

'But as it turned out, you didn't have to?'

'Right,' he said. 'Mr Talmascy was here for some sort of business with those two policemen.'

'Watkins and Brady.'

'Uh-huh. And they were chummy.'

'You didn't connect Mr Talmascy's visits with the turnover in the service staff?'

He looked away, like it was taking every ounce of his brain power to answer my question.

'You know,' he said, like he'd discovered penicillin, 'I think you're right! Do you think this Mr Talmascy could be a union organizer?'

'When do you go back to FSU?' I asked him. 'When's this alleged internship over?'

'End of the month.'

'How often do they send someone from your program to the Benton?'

'Every semester,' he said. 'And I was lucky to get it. My grades aren't very good. I failed Hospitality Leadership and Ethics twice, and made a D in International Wine and Culture, so I have to take it over again.'

I tried to be sympathetic. 'Too much drinking; not enough notes.'

'Exactly!' he agreed.

'So, this Mr Talmascy . . .'

'Not much more to tell.' He lowered his voice. 'Except that he was drunk the last time I saw him here.'

'What made you think that?'

'He was crying. Most big men don't cry like that unless they're drunk.'

'I see. He was alone?'

'With the cops. They looked like they were made out of wood. You know, stiff. Not happy.'

'And he's gone now.'

'Haven't seen him since that night,' he concluded. 'Were you really going to arrest me?'

I shook my head. 'You know I wasn't.'

'You–you're a lot nicer than the cops, aren't you?'

'Yes,' I agreed. 'I am.'

He'd said that because of my sudden change of tune. Instead of pressing my 'I have handcuffs' gambit, I'd asked him about himself. Where'd he go to college; what was he studying? You never go wrong getting people to talk about themselves.

'Oh!' Tim snapped. 'Hey! Will this help?'

He reached under the desk and produced a small envelope.

I stared down at the envelope. 'What is it?'

'Mr Talmascy's American Express card. He left it at the bar in there. I was just going to hold it here until, you know, the next time he came back.'

I picked up the envelope. 'I don't know if it'll help or not, but if you let me take it away right now, I promise to bring it back to you by tomorrow.'

'Sure.' The kid shrugged. 'I don't think he even knows it's gone. He hasn't called about it or anything. You'll bring it back, right?'

I nodded and pocketed the envelope. 'By the way, still no sign of the Seminole kid I was asking you about?'

'Sorry.' And he was.

'You don't mind if I look around upstairs?'

He nodded. 'You want a pass key?'

Tim was my new friend. Tim held out a pass key.

'I'll bring it *right* back,' I told him, taking the key.

All I could think to myself was *John Horse is really going to be impressed with me the next time I see him, considering all the answers I got.*

Unfortunately, strolling around upstairs in the Benton was a waste of time, and ended up bringing me down a little bit. The Cuban maids weren't talkative. The pass key didn't do me any good. What was I going to do – bust into every room? And no sign of the kid anywhere, despite twice humiliating myself by hollering, 'Duck!'

When I went back downstairs, Tim wasn't at the desk. I

dropped off the pass key and headed out the door. I thought about going to the hospital to check in with Sharp, but it seemed to me that finding this Talmascy character was more to the point.

For that, all I needed was a phone and a little time; hence I took myself back to my pad, and got on the horn as soon as I walked in the door.

'Hello, yes,' I murmured to the American Express agent, glancing at the card. 'My name is Bear Litka Talmascy and I think my card has been stolen.'

It took three full minutes to convince her that the first name on the card was *Bear*, and then I had to spell Talmascy twice. I called out the number on the card, and she took a while.

'Last used,' she said, 'at the Benton Inn in Fly's Bay, Florida.'

'*Fry's* Bay,' I corrected. 'Yes, and before that was probably Oklahoma in the—'

'New York,' she interrupted. 'LaBracca Pizza.'

I couldn't stop myself from sucking in a little breath. LaBracca Pizza was a wise-guy establishment in Manhattan, the kind that even my pals in Brooklyn were afraid of. I covered by saying, 'Right. LaBracca's. Look, don't cancel the card, I'm still in Florida. I'll just pop over to the Benton and pick it up. But I'm on the road and I don't want you to send the newest bill to my home address. Could you forward it to where I'm staying in Florida? I want to check to see if anyone at the Benton has abused my card, you understand.'

'I can send it today, if you like,' she said with absolutely no affect.

'Perfect.' I gave her Yudda's address. 'Can you put a rush on it? I'm anxious.'

'I'll do my best, sir. Is there anything else I can help you with?'

'As a matter of fact, yes. When you send the regular bill, it's to my home address in Oklahoma City, right? Not the business one? Sorry, you wouldn't believe how long I've been on the road. I'm a little addled.'

'The home address, sir,' she said without a trace of sympathy for Mr Talmascy's travails. 'Oklahoma City.'

'You've been very helpful,' I assured her, and then I hung up.
A nice bit of bluffing, I thought. I knew where the guy was
from, where he'd been before he came to Fry's Bay and just
how scary he might be. Now all I had to do was suss out the
exact address for the guy in Oklahoma City.

And once again I was happy with my hunches and impressed
with my luck. Life was a roller coaster, really.

All I had to do then was figure out why a Seminole named
Bear would visit LaBracca Pizza in Manhattan.

TWELVE

I sat in my kitchen contemplating my next move. I was torn. Duck was missing and I had to find him. Talmascy was the devil I had to catch. But my heart really wanted to find out who killed Pan Pan. I had done my best to keep Pan Pan out of my mind. I couldn't bring myself to believe he was dead.

Once he came over to my house for Passover Seder. My aunt insisted. She and my mother cooked for three days beforehand, and Pan Pan worried for five. He was afraid he was going to do or say something wrong. He didn't realize that, after the religious rigmarole, my mother and my aunt were both Lenny Bruce: filthy and hilarious.

He showed up in a new suit with a bouquet of flowers that set him back a hundred bucks. And he didn't say a word for the first thirty minutes, just nodded or shook his head. When my aunt explained that there was an empty seat at the table just in case Elijah stopped by, he kept staring at it like there was a ghost in the chair.

Then my aunt started talking about eating matzo and bitter herbs to remind us of slavery. Pan Pan leaned over to me and whispered, 'When were *you* guys slaves?'

My aunt stopped her little speech, looked at Pan Pan over her glasses and said, 'You think you people had it hard after the Emancipation Proclamation? At least they didn't ship you to Death Valley and make you wander around for forty years afterward!'

For some reason that cracked him up and he started laughing like a maniac. Part of it was nerves. But my aunt was well pleased with herself because she'd worked the audience, and the rest of the night was smooth sailing.

At the door, when he was leaving, he said to me, 'Do you think I could come over to dinner again sometime? My family – I mean, I was raised by an aunt too, but she don't cook nothing but skag and she's usually holed up with a trick around suppertime, so. It feels good in your home.'

He was right. It did feel good.

A knock on my door shook me out of my memories. Given the temperature of the situation in general, I was wary.

'Who is it?' I called out, trying to sound like a tough.

A little voice answered. 'Foggy?'

I got to the door quick; there stood Duck. He looked up at me. He'd been crying.

'I've been looking for you,' I told him. 'Where you been?'

He didn't answer.

'Where's my sister?' he asked me.

'In the hospital. Somebody beat her up.'

He took that news oddly. 'I found my mother's scarf. Me and my sister bought it for her one time and she never takes it off. Even when it's too hot to wear it. I found it in the dumpster behind the hotel. I think my mother is dead.'

He steeled himself and stared at me like a Seminole warrior. Then he held out the scarf. It was nice. Label said Hermès. It was kind of a forest scene, with lots of birds. Mostly owls.

'She's not dead,' I told him, and I sounded a lot more certain than I felt. 'We already decided she was taken as a part of some sort of human-trafficking ring. They don't kill people, those guys. The whole gig is to have live people to traffic, right?'

'My sister,' he began.

'She's asleep. She found something too. John Horse said it was owl demons or something.'

'Oh.' He closed his eyes and his whole face changed. 'Stikini. That makes me feel better. *They* took this off her, because they didn't want anyone to know they were evil beings. The owls were a clue.'

I didn't have the heart to disagree with him, because he did seem to feel better.

'So, let's go to the hospital and see about your sister,' I said.

I didn't offer my hand, he just took it. And just like that, he wasn't a Seminole warrior any more. He was a little kid again, worried about his mother.

*   *   *

At the hospital, John Horse was sleeping in a chair beside
Sharp's bed. Sharp was still out. Duck went right to her side,
took her hand and started whispering something or other.
That made John Horse's eyes open, and when he saw
me he sat up.

'You found out something,' he said.

'Do you know anything about a guy who calls himself
Bear Talmascy?' I asked.

John Horse slumped down. 'Oh.'

I could tell by the look on his face that Talmascy was
bad news.

'You've heard the name,' I assumed.

He glanced over at the unconscious kid. 'She was right.
Owl demon.'

I tried not to sound too indulgent. 'OK, but besides being
an owl, he's also from Oklahoma City. Where is it that your
relatives always got shipped off to?'

'The Seminole Tribal Jurisdiction Area is about an hour east
of Oklahoma City; the Tribal Complex is in Wewoka.'

'Didn't you tell me you'd been there?'

'Long time ago. It's right at the junction of US 270 and
Oklahoma Highway 56.'

His voice sounded tired.

'I know it's a sore spot, the way you were moved out of
Florida.'

He grimaced. '*Sore spot?* Treaty of Moultrie Creek in 1823,
the government made us give up all our land except for a
reservation in the center of Florida, where my village is now.
But that wasn't enough for these whites. They wanted us all
moved out. In 1832, in the springtime, we were called to a
meeting at Payne's Landing on the Oklawaha River. It was
a secret meeting, with no record, and they wanted us to move
in with the Creeks. We're not Creeks. So they told us to
go to Oklahoma. Many people went there. Many stayed here.
Do you know how to destroy a culture? Chop it in half. Each
half might survive, but it's broken after that. Not the same.'

That was the longest speech John Horse had ever given,
as far as I could remember. And his voice was as bitter – it
occurred to me – as the herbs at a Passover Seder.

'My point was,' I said, as gently as I could, 'that maybe we should try to summon up this Bear Talmascy and see if he can put his hand to the mother of these two kids, since I'm pretty sure he had everything to do with her disappearance.'

'Where is he now, Talmascy?'

'No idea,' I admitted. 'But get a load of this: before he came to Fry's Bay around the time the mother got nabbed, he was in New York at a wise-guy club.'

His eyes got big. 'He was with the mafia?'

'Please!' I snapped. 'We don't like to say it out like that. But . . . he *was* probably visiting with some members of a certain family.'

'We don't like to say the name of the owl demons out loud,' he said, smiling, 'because it might make you turn into one. You do the same: you don't call them what they are so that you won't become one of their number.'

'No,' I objected. 'It's just rude, like belching at the dinner table or dogging a guy's wife at his funeral.'

John Horse shook his head. 'White manners. I'll never understand them.'

'Fine. Could we skip the discussion of etiquette, then, and move on? I have a sincere desire to find this Talmascy character.'

'You think he might be back in Oklahoma?'

'The idea I have in my head is that he's the one who convinces the Seminole women to abscond,' I said, 'and then the police take over and ship them off.'

'Where? Why? Does it have anything to do with the Oklahoma Seminoles? And also, does it have to do with . . . a certain family in New York?'

'Now you're on my wavelength.'

He stood up. 'I don't know what that means, but we should probably go. I'm glad you found the boy.'

He glanced over at Duck.

'Turned out to be fairly easy,' I admitted. 'He found his mother's scarf in the dumpster behind the Benton.'

John Horse nodded. 'The one with the owls on it. You see how events conspire to tell you a story if you just pay attention? Now we know for certain that Talmascy was involved.'

I didn't want to fuel his whole mystical Seminole fire, so I just nodded instead of telling him how much of my instinct I had to use to put two and two together.

'Duck,' I said. 'Stay here, and I mean it. Stay with your sister until I come back. All right?'

'She's in the other world,' he said, not looking at me. 'She's trying to find our mother using her abilities to see things that can't be seen. Isn't that right?'

'Yes,' John Horse said instantly. 'It is.'

'And we're going to wander around in this world to do the same thing,' I added, 'so stay here.'

'I will,' he promised.

'I already spoke with Maggie Redhawk,' I told him. 'She's going to watch out for you while I'm gone; fix you up with a little bed right here in this room. Will you be OK?'

He tilted his head in my direction. 'Not really. My mother's missing and my sister's in a coma.'

What could I say?

He returned his attention to his sister. John Horse and I headed for the door.

When we were in the hall, John Horse said, 'You've done very well in a short time. How did you find out about Talmascy?'

'Like always,' I shrugged, 'a combination of brains, intuition and blind, stupid luck.'

'It's not stupid luck,' he said. 'You can always find a path, and when you do, you walk on it. That's why I like you.'

'Yeah.' I lowered my voice. 'But here's what I just started thinking: what if my *path* takes me to Oklahoma? Or worse: back to New York?'

He grinned. 'Then I'm coming with you. I never been in New York. I don't think anything I heard about it is true. And I have relatives in Oklahoma, of course. It will be a great trip. I like riding in that fancy car of yours.'

'Hold on,' I said. 'Nobody's taking the T-bird on a road trip. I was just kind of wondering out loud. And anyway, if I *do* go, I'll be going alone.'

'Oh.' He sounded genuinely disappointed.

'And we have plenty to do here before I go traipsing off anywhere else.'

'The death of your friend,' he said, 'and the man who killed him.'

'That's just it,' I told him. 'I don't see why Icepick would kill Pan Pan. And I certainly don't understand why Icepick would drive a car we sold him all the way to Florida to dump Pan Pan's body in our little bay. There are twenty-seven places to dump a body within walking distance of where Pan Pan lives, for God's sake.'

'Doesn't sound like a very nice neighborhood,' John Horse observed.

'It's not, but that's beside the point.'

He nodded. 'Somebody else killed your friend and Icepick wanted you to know about it.'

'That's more likely. I mean, it's not the sort of thing you'd write a letter about. Icepick would never be so dopey as to use the phone for such a thing.'

'One of your other friends wouldn't call you, though?' he ventured.

'As I have told you on many occasions,' I answered, a little irritated by the question, 'no one's supposed to know where I am. I'm sort of on the lam. And *plus*, now that I'm quasi-legit, the pals who *could* find out where I am would not care for the fact that I'm like a sort of cop.'

He nodded again. 'Your life is complex.'

'Like you wouldn't believe,' I agreed. 'So, first let me deal with the things I can deal with simply, OK?'

'OK. Like what?'

I headed toward the police station. 'Like finding out what's really going on with the crooked cops in this town. Maybe you shouldn't come with me. I'm going into the station full of guesses and made-up threats.'

He picked up his pace. 'Great! That should be fun.'

I was in luck. Brady and Watkins were the only ones in the police station when John Horse and I barged through the front door.

Going once again for the bold approach, I let them have it.

'The thing is,' I shouted, 'I know that both of you are involved with Bear Talmascy in kidnapping Seminole women, and I've turned over my findings to the FBI. *Man*, are they ever going to be on your ass. I just came down to watch them take you away!'

John Horse stepped back. He didn't want to be anywhere near me when the counter-threats started making their way around the room.

'Listen, Moscowitz . . .' Brady growled.

I interrupted. 'I *know* what's going on, jackass. I have hard evidence. I know Talmascy, see. He's a part of my circle up in New York. Get it? My *circle*.'

It was a reasonable bluff. If Bear had been in LaBracca's he was dealing with the organization in some way or another. And if Brady was in on it, he'd know that too.

Brady stared into my eyes like he was trying to read a difficult page of physics.

At that moment, Watkins stood up.

'Foggy,' he said calmly, 'what do you think you're doing? You're interfering with police business. We told you. We're on the case about the missing women. It's all under control. Seriously. You should leave.'

'I probably should,' I said, 'but, unfortunately, I take my job seriously. No one is more surprised about that than I am, by the way.'

'I see,' Watkins said. 'Nothing I can do to make you back off?'

'You could kill me.'

Watkins took in a deep breath, and when he let it out, he was a different person. His entire demeanor had changed. His face didn't even look human for a second.

'OK, then,' Watkins said. 'I don't know what you think you know, but it doesn't matter. Go ahead, Brady. You're up.'

Brady nodded grimly. 'He means I get to take care of you, see? I've been looking forward to this since I got to town.'

He took out his pistol.

'What do you think, Foggy?' Watkins asked, coming around his desk. 'Should we say that you were shot attacking a police officer, or shot trying to escape custody?'

I glanced over at John Horse. He was a statue.

'What about the witness here?' I asked.

'I don't see any witness,' Watkins rumbled. 'I see a crazy old man nobody in town takes seriously. I think he's probably retarded.'

John Horse still didn't move or speak.

'He's the leader of a thousand angry Seminole men who live within walking distance of this office,' I countered. 'He gives the word, and you're Custer.'

Watkins rolled his head.

'Then I guess we'll just have to kill him too,' he said impatiently. 'Either way, it's time to finish you off. Now, Brady.'

Brady raised his gun, smiling.

'This is going to be fun,' he said loudly.

'Not in the office, moron!' Watkins snapped. 'Take them over to Blake Road. Where we found the kids. Let the patrol guys find them in a day or two.'

Brady's grin got bigger. 'By the smell.'

I considered the cliché that goes: 'Run from a knife but rush a gun.' But just as I was about to move, I saw something in Brady's eyes. Something I'd never seen there before. For about two seconds, he looked like an actual human being.

So, I thought, I could rush him just as good in the alley as I could in the station house. Let's see what he's got in mind.

I backed away from Brady's gun; made a little gesture to John Horse. He nodded. We both moved toward the back door of the station house.

The second we were out behind the station house, Brady lowered his gun and eyeballed me.

'You gotta get out of town, right?' he said. 'You and John Horse. You got no idea what's really going on here. If you know anything about Talmascy, follow up with that. But not here in Fry's Bay. Here, you're dead, got it?'

I didn't understand, but I nodded.

He glanced up at John Horse. 'You too. I mean it.'

John Horse shrugged. 'We were going to go to New York anyway.'

Brady didn't know what to make of that. He just put his gun away and walked out of the alley toward Blake Road.

'Then you'd better move fast,' he said over his shoulder. 'Because, I repeat, you're dead in Fry's Bay.'

THIRTEEN

On the road

Before we went for my car, John Horse insisted on stopping by the hospital. We took the back way, stayed out of sight. We caught up with Maggie Redhawk in the hallway.

'I'm worried about Topalargee and her brother,' John Horse told her. 'Worried about their safety. There's something going on here that I don't understand.'

She shook her head. 'You got no worries there. I already called my brother.'

End of story. Mister Redhawk – a guy whose parents were so serious about respect that they named their first-born male child *Mister* – was a Seminole power player. Rich, good looking, politically influential, a snappy dresser and, when it counted, well-armed. If he was looking out for the kids, they were in the pocket, safe and sound. Load off my mind.

Still, I had to see them before I left town.

Duck was still standing at his sister's bedside, holding her hand, staring at her face. He heard us come in but didn't look away from her.

'She's trying to tell me something,' he said.

John Horse went to stand beside him. 'What is she trying to say?'

'For an hour, she's been mumbling something about having pizza in Oklahoma. Maggie Redhawk said she was delirious, but I think she's got information.'

John Horse glanced in my direction.

I nodded. 'I don't know how she figured it, but that sounds an awful lot like Talmascy's connection, right? New York pizza joint to Oklahoma Seminole Reservation?'

'That's what it sounds like to me,' John Horse agreed.

'She's in the other world,' Duck said reverentially, 'and she can see things that we can't.'

'Or,' John Horse said, in an uncharacteristically straightforward moment, 'she heard something in the bakery building that gave her a clue. Maybe she confronted someone, and that *someone* beat her up, or tried to kill her. And her last conscious effort was to construct the owl-demon icon.'

'*Now* you're choosing to play it straight with me?' I asked him. 'No shaman horse manure?'

He grinned. 'I'm dead, remember? I *have* to be honest now.'

'The dead have to be honest?' I shook my head. 'That's a new one on me. But look, is it possible that this Talmascy guy was there in the bakery? Is still here in Fry's Bay?'

'It's possible,' he admitted.

Maggie Redhawk had been standing in the doorway, nervously watching the hall.

'Look,' she said softly, 'you two got to go now. If the cops hear that you were in this room, there's trouble all the way around.'

'She's right,' I agreed. 'We should *amscray*.'

John Horse nodded.

Then he put his hand on Duck's shoulder. 'She's going to be fine. We're going to find your mother. And I made some turtle stew. It's at Foggy's house. In the refrigerator.'

'When did you make turtle stew in my house?' I asked him.

'Same time I made breakfast. Let's go.'

We slipped out a service exit, stuck to the shadows and made it back to my place in no time. I gathered a few essentials while John Horse kept watch, and then we both got into my T-bird and took the long way out of town. By the time we were on I-95 headed north, the sun was beginning to head west, thinking about a dip in the Pacific Ocean.

Now, the drive from Florida to New York was a long one. Not something you could do all at once. John Horse, as usual, had no money. My own wallet was a little light too. And all my money was going to have to go to gas. I could get some more green once I got to New York, but in the meantime, where was food? Where was a motel?

John Horse came up with a couple of nefarious solutions that I rejected, because I was doing my best to stay on the straight side of the new leaf I'd turned over since coming to Florida.

I explained to him that if I drove eight hours a day, which was a stretch for both of us in my little car, it would be a three-day trip. We needed someplace to stay for two nights, and something to eat for at least six meals.

So, before we left Florida, John Horse made me stop at a farm stand. He managed to trade a fancy Seminole bracelet he was wearing for a dozen hen-house eggs and some smoked bacon slabs. It was a pretty good deal for the farmer. The bacon and eggs were worth three dollars; the farmer could sell the bracelet for ten. But there we were: breakfast solved, as long as you didn't mind eating food cooked on a hot stone, Seminole style.

Supper was the challenge, until I remembered that Savannah, Georgia, was home to Congregation Mickve Israel, one of the oldest Temples in the United States. Organized around 1735 by the Sephardim – Spanish-Portuguese side of the family. And Savannah was right on our way.

A little fast talking, a little Yiddish – as best I could remember it – and Bob was our collective uncle: two boiled chickens and enough matzo to last for forty years.

In this way, we were able to stutter forward. Long days of hypnotic driving, with John Horse insisting on AM radio. I thought if I heard 'Boogie Fever' or 'Disco Lady' one more time I was going to pull my radio out of the dashboard and throw it on to the highway. Along with John Horse.

The first night we stayed at the Skyliner, a motel with no view of anything that looked like a skyline. John Horse slept on the floor.

The second night we pulled into a rest area and took turns sleeping in the car with the seats shoved back as far as we could get them. John Horse ate candy bars from a vending machine.

And on the third day, we arrived in New York, only a little the less for wear.

John Horse was ecstatic. Since I-95 ran right through

Manhattan, he was getting more of a look at the city than he could take in. After a while he closed his eyes.

'How did you live here for so long?' he asked me.

'I didn't live *here*,' I explained. 'I lived in Brooklyn.'

But the fact was I found myself just as overwhelmed as he was. Too much noise, too many lights, chaos everywhere. My sad realization was that I didn't belong in Florida, but I couldn't really come back to New York any more. I suddenly felt all kinds of homeless.

So, I focused on the goal: pop in at LaBracca Pizza, ask about Talmascy and get the hell out of town, on the way to Oklahoma.

Now, just walking into LaBracca's wasn't the smartest thing to do, but the fact was that, thanks to pals like Red Levine, I had a rep, minor as it was. I was the one that got away, absconded from New York ahead of the cops and disappeared in the vapor. And I was also a kind of crook Robin Hood because I sent money every month to a certain kid, no strings attached. My every-day Yom Kippur. The kid was well-cared-for.

But I digress. There we were, sitting in front of LaBracca's at around ten in the evening, staring at the black door – and the goon in front of that door.

'I think you should wait here,' I told John Horse.

'You think I should have waited in Florida,' he mumbled.

'Right. Back in a flash.' I took my pistol, holster and all, out of the neat little place in the small of my back and put it in John Horse's lap. 'Just in case.'

'Don't you need it?' he asked me.

I shook my head. 'If I go waving a gun around in there, it'll only make these guys laugh.'

With that, I hoisted myself out of the car and on to the dirty sidewalk. LaBracca's was in a less fashionable part of the city, the wrong end of the Meatpacking District. They kept saying the area was up and coming. But it was 1976, and there just didn't seem to be much movement in that direction.

This particular street looked abandoned, but I figured it was that most people didn't want to disturb the denizens of LaBracca's, which I was just about to do.

Deep breath; straighten my tie.

Before I got within ten feet of the goon at the door, he rumbled, 'Keep walking, pal.'

'My name is Foggy Moscowitz,' I said in a loud, clear voice, 'and I came all the way from Florida to ask, with great respect, three questions of anyone who might be enjoying an evening at LaBracca's right now.'

The guy tilted his head and gave me a very thorough gander.

'You're Foggy Moscowitz?'

'I'm going to reach around to my hip pocket and take out my wallet,' I explained without moving a muscle. 'That way I can show you my driver's license and you can be sure.'

He nodded once. I moved like a glacier, got out my wallet and produced my ID.

He stared at it, and then at me, for a full minute.

'This ought to be interesting,' he said quietly.

Then he stood aside and opened the door.

The place was under-lit and silent as the grave. When I got past the door frame I could see about ten tables. Only one was occupied. Three guys. Two of them were bodyguards – you could tell by the way they were sitting.

'This is Foggy Moscowitz,' the doorman announced. 'All the way from Florida.'

The man in between the two bodyguards leaned forward. His face was pockmarked and he had a lazy eye, but his suit cost as much as my car.

'May I come in?' I asked.

The man nodded once.

I took eight or ten steps, and stopped about three yards away from the table.

'You know that Red Levine is a kind of uncle to me,' I began.

'I know who you are,' he interrupted me. 'Everybody in town knows the name. It's an honor to have you in our establishment. Unless you have come to steal my car.'

There was a moment of silence, and then the guy cracked up. Which in turn encouraged his guys to laugh. And I was forced to smile as well.

'I have come, with the utmost respect, to ask you three questions,' I said when the hilarity simmered down.

The man heaved a heavy sigh. 'I think I know why you're here.'

You had to be very careful about a statement like that. You didn't want to disagree; you didn't want to give anything away.

'Then, with respect, can you help me?'

'Not directly,' he said, refusing to look at me. 'Because the business to which you refer is financed, in part, by my friends. But it's a dirty business, and I am not surprised that you are concerned about it. That's one question.'

'But you can help me indirectly,' I said slowly, careful not to make it sound like a question.

He nodded.

'All right,' I said, 'before I ask that question, let me ask you this: if I pursue this situation in Florida, will I ruffle anybody's feathers?'

He seemed to think for a moment, and then he said, 'Not mine. And to my knowledge, no one in New York will care if you make things right in Florida. This is not a business concern of ours, you understand. We were merely the bankroll. And we're supposed to be paid back with interest. So, that would conclude our understanding with all parties, you understand.'

'Good,' I told him, 'because I would never wish to show anything but the greatest deference to your interests.'

He sniffed.

'So, my final question is this,' I said. 'Is it possible that your indirect help could come in the form of a name or an address?'

'Yes.'

He whispered something to one of his guys. The guy got up. I planted my feet, waiting for anything. But the guy walked right past me and behind the bar in the joint.

'Tony is fixing a little espresso to go for you and your Indian friend,' he said. 'You look tired.'

How he knew that John Horse was out in the car was a mystery I did not wish to ask about.

All I said was, 'It is indeed a long drive from Florida to Manhattan.'

His response was, for a moment, nonsense.

'Pody Poe,' he said.

I stood silent for a minute.

'Tracy Coy Poe,' he went on, by way of explanation. 'In Oklahoma City.'

'Oh.' I tried very hard not to respond any more than that.

Poe was an Oklahoma gambler, a famous guy in our circles. I was surprised I hadn't thought of him. His father was a songwriter and his mother was a judge's daughter. Spent the Depression years in Hollywood with his father, working at MGM. They had some sort of falling out with Bing Crosby, and that was that. Poe ended up playing pool in Oklahoma, and he was good at it. Good enough to eventually build a very nice criminal empire there. Nice enough, in fact, that Nixon's recent Organized Crime Control Act spent millions of dollars trying to get him. In short, he was in trouble. But they hadn't gotten him yet.

'*That* Pody Poe,' I said after a moment.

I looked at my host, and realized I wasn't getting anything more out of him. His guy came from behind the bar and handed me a paper bag.

'It's got tops,' he told me, 'but still, be careful not to spill. Best espresso in New York.'

'Thank you very much,' I said, taking the bag. 'This will certainly hit the spot. Look, you also don't care what happens to Mr Talmascy, do you?'

My nameless host smiled.

'You have used up your three questions,' he said quietly, 'but since I have no idea who Bear Talmascy is, what do I care what you do to him?'

I took a step backward. 'You have been a godsend, may I say? And I will not forget your kindness to me.'

He stuck out his lower lip. 'I think it would be better if you did forget it. It is my plan to forget that you were ever in New York. For the security of all concerned.'

'Ah,' I answered him. 'Agreed.'

I continued to back away, still facing him.

'Hey, Foggy,' the guy called out, and his voice was very different. 'I don't know if this will mean anything to you or not, but I knew your father. Slightly. He would be very proud of you.'

Since I did *not* know my father, even slightly, it really didn't matter at all to me. But I wasn't about to insult the guy. So I came up with, 'You have no idea what that means to me.'

Which was certainly true.

I backed into the doorframe and the door opened like magic.

'Goodnight, Mr Moscowitz,' the doorman said. 'Safe travels to Oklahoma.'

And then the guy handed me a couple of Jacksons. Out of nowhere. I started to say something, but he turned away from me and shook his head, so I just nodded.

'Thank you,' I said, and made for my car.

John Horse was singing when I handed him an espresso. Not some Seminole mystic thing, either. He was singing 'Play That Funky Music, White Boy'. Very softly. It was another song that was big on the radio, for reasons that escaped all human understanding.

When I cranked up the car, he stopped singing.

'How did it go?' he asked me.

'Great. We're going to Oklahoma City.'

He shifted in his seat. 'No. We just got to New York. I haven't seen anything yet. I want to see the Empire State building. And the Statue of Liberty. I want to see that show, "Oh! Calcutta!" It's got naked people in it.'

I took a very deep breath. 'I have told you on no fewer than seven occasions that I am still on the wanted list in New York. It's been a few years, but escaping police custody isn't really something that these guys like to forget. Every second I stay in this burg is a second closer to a jail cell. All it's going to take is one guy saying, "Hey, Foggy's back in town!" And I'm a goner. Do you understand that?'

He looked at me for a long time. 'I can see that you're all wound up. I think that looking at naked people on a theatrical stage would make you feel better.'

I nosed my T-bird out on to the street. 'I think that a trip on Route 66 would make me feel better. We'll pick it up in St Louis.'

'I love that song.' He settled back in his seat and began singing, 'If you ever plan to motor west . . .'

Now, Route 66 was certainly a famous highway, and Nat King Cole's song about it was, likewise, a snappy tune. Much better than 'Play that Funky Music, White Boy'. But I did not even begin to feel like singing until we were out of Manhattan and past Newark.

After John Horse sang 'Route 66' three times, he went to sleep, which was a blessing.

When he woke up we were somewhere just before Columbus, not quite eight hours later.

'Where are we?' he asked me, stretching.

'Ohio.'

'You been driving a long time.'

'We'll stop in Indianapolis,' I told him. 'Give me a stretch and a bite to eat. At a diner, by the way. No more stone-cooked eggs. I got forty bucks from the doorman at LaBracca's.'

His eyes widened. 'You did? What for?'

'I told you,' I assured him. 'I got a rep.'

But, in truth, I was just as baffled as John Horse was.

FOURTEEN

The outskirts of Indianapolis were a little like the garbage dump outside of John Horse's Seminole village, but on Yudda's recommendation, I took a little detour to the east side of town and parked at the Steer-In, fine food since 1960. It was a low, square building with a kind of turquoise strip along the top and at the entrance, and a lot of glass in front.

They served breakfast all day.

But I ordered two Twin Steer burgers, the coleslaw and a whole cream pie. John Horse got steak and eggs, a Belgian waffle and corned beef hash. And by the time I paid the tab, I was pretty sure we'd destroyed at least two pots of coffee.

Out in the parking lot, I was, unfortunately, attacked by a moment of reflection. Turned out that my first time back to the City since I'd absconded gave me a sting of melancholy like you wouldn't believe. I realized how much I missed New York. Thank God, I thought, I didn't visit Brooklyn, and my mother, like I'd wanted to. I'd have been crying out loud.

New York wasn't just a place to be born, see, or Brooklyn a borough to grow up in. To me, it was an invisible tattoo that you lived with, no matter where else you went. You missed the city even when you didn't know it, and it was on your mind no matter what else you were thinking. Hidden under every light-hearted moment in Fry's Bay there was a heavy dose of wanting something or other in Brooklyn. Every beautiful sunset over the ocean out my back door in Florida was only a mask of the lights on Broadway.

And suddenly, at that moment, in a parking lot in Indianapolis, you couldn't have made me feel any worse if you'd taken a gun and shot me. That's the amount of lonesome I was.

John Horse figured that out, of course. Just by looking at my face, I guess. He leaned against the T-Bird, arms folded, staring out at the parked cars.

'Human beings are, by nature, nomads,' he said, not looking at me. 'So, it's a curious thing that we miss any place we call *home*.'

'But we do,' I said.

'Would you believe it?' he asked me. 'I miss my crappy little cinderblock house out there in the swamp. Worst place anybody could ever live, and I wish I could go there right now and lie down and rest. Even though, I have to say, I'm enjoying this road trip more than anything I've done in years.'

'It's a curious thing,' I repeated. 'Home.'

'That's why you didn't want to stay in the city,' he said. 'Not because you were afraid of getting caught, but because it hurt too much to be there.'

I rolled my head and got into the car. 'OK, Doctor Freud. Next I'd like to know why I let some looney ancient Seminole come along with me on this trip.'

'That's not psychological,' he said, getting into the driver's seat. 'That's practical. You need me when you go to deal with those Oklahoma Seminoles. *They're* crazy.'

The outskirts of Oklahoma City were, in my opinion, very dusty. I had determined that if my friend at LaBracca's wanted me to check in with Pody Poe before I did anything in the state, I had probably better listen to that advice.

There were plenty of places he might have been, but since it was the middle of the afternoon on Wednesday, I decided to start with a mini golf place called Hook 'N' Slice. Poe owned it and hung out there sometimes. I had no idea where it was, so I stopped at a Shell station to ask.

Before the man could speak, John Horse made a strange pronouncement.

'Did you know that Oklahoma City has a female mayor?' John Horse asked me. 'Her name is Patience Latting. She's in favor of tearing down historic old buildings to put up skyscrapers. It isn't working out so well. They got vacant lots everywhere.'

The man at the gas pump at the Shell station volunteered his own opinion.

'We're about to build a huge botanical garden right in the middle of town,' he told us pointedly.

'Yeah, I just want to play a little miniature golf,' I said. 'So – Hook 'N' Slice?'

He gave me the eye. I was wearing the shiny gray sharkskin suit with the thin black tie, completely out of step with his disco jump suit. He put two and two together right away.

'Poe's place. Yeah.'

And he offered a terse set of directions without looking me in the eye.

As we pulled out of the station, I asked John Horse, 'Did you deliberately egg that guy on with your urban ruination statement?'

'Yes.' He smiled.

'Why?'

'Wanted to see where he stood.'

'And where, exactly, did he stand?' I asked.

'Beside your car,' he told me, like I was a dope, 'in a gas station.'

I knew he was getting at something. He usually was. I just didn't want to play with him; I wanted to get ready to talk to a guy who was hooked up with a guy who would kill me if I asked the wrong questions. I'd been in that same situation plenty when I lived in Brooklyn, but I knew I was rusty from a couple of years in Florida. Wise-guy speak was a very subtle language, the nuances of which could get a person iced if he wasn't careful.

This was, of course, assuming Mr Poe was in situ at the Hook 'N' Slice.

So, I followed the directions and ended up at the course in no time. There were people playing, and it was a sunny day.

John Horse got out and wandered. I went to the admission kiosk.

'Hello,' I said to the teenaged girl at the counter. 'My name is Moscowitz and I was hoping to speak with Mr Poe. Is he in, by any chance?'

She stared into my eyes like she was about to read my future, the most intense gaze I'd endured in a very long time.

'Mr Poe is indisposed,' she said.

The name tag said *Rita*. Her voice was husky. She had black eyeliner, a shag haircut and big hoops in her ears. And she was wearing a mood ring. It was dark blue. It took me a second longer to notice the Adam's apple. She was a he.

I smiled. 'I'm from Brooklyn. Where Lou Reed was born.'

'So?' Rita asked.

'I'm just wondering how difficult it is to take a walk on the wild side here in Oklahoma City.'

That handed Rita a laugh.

'I *love* that song.'

'I'm more a Charlie Parker fan,' I admitted.

'"Walk on the Wild Side" has a nice sax part in it,' Rita said.

'Does indeed. So, Mr Poe is *indisposed.*'

'Yeah,' Rita assured me, 'but he knew you were coming. I was getting to that. He said to give this to you if you showed up. And here you are. Visiting fireman.'

Rita slid me a thick envelope.

When I picked it up, Rita leaned forward. 'Don't open it here.'

I put it in my suit coat pocket.

'Planning to stick around for long?' Rita asked me, eyebrows arched.

'Depends on what's in this envelope.'

'Well, see,' Rita said, one shoulder up, 'I thought you might like to find out what the wild side of the city looks like. You know. At night.'

'It's a lovely offer,' I said. 'But I'm not your guy.'

I hesitated because I saw the hurt look in Rita's eyes.

'I'm too old for you,' I said. 'I'd be, like, your grandpa at some disco.'

A little assuaged, Rita sighed. '*Dommage.*'

And that was that.

I sidled up to John Horse. He was watching, with great amusement, as Caucasians played miniature golf. The field was laid out with maybe eighteen holes at various angles. There were paths in between, and lights overhead, on even in the bright Oklahoma sunshine. It was, to me, a bizarre imitation of an imitation of nature, the waste of a perfectly good vacant lot.

'It's a very funny game,' he said to me.

'Incomprehensible to me,' I admitted.

There was a man in pressed slacks and a crisp white shirt trying to hit the ball down a stretch of green carpet toward a hole the size of a softball. He wasn't having much luck, and it seemed to be making him very upset.

'What's in the envelope?' he asked me. 'I saw the girl give it to you.'

I looked down at it. 'Let's have a look.'

I tore open the envelope and there were ten Grants wrapped in a rubber band along with a slip of paper that said, '*Tecumseh.*' That was all.

'Everybody's giving me money,' I whispered. 'Five hundred bucks here.'

John Horse glanced at the name on the paper and sniffed, then made a beeline for the car.

'Eddie Harjo,' he said.

I stared. 'Who?'

'We're going to Seminole County. Come on.'

Seminole County was a little more than an hour southeast of Oklahoma City. Before Oklahoma was a state, the area was chosen as the repository of all the Seminoles who were taken from Florida in the 1820s.

But in 1923, oil was discovered there. Thirty-nine different oil pools. By 1929 the area produced nearly two hundred million barrels of oil a year. Drove the price of oil all the way up to seventeen cents a barrel. Doesn't take much to figure what the Seminoles got out of all that.

We were out of Oklahoma City and into a lot of low scrub before John Horse spoke again.

'Do you remember my telling you about the Treaty of Moultrie Creek?'

'Where you guys got screwed out of a bunch of land.' I nodded.

'In 1961, we filed a claim to be compensated for that land. It took them until this year, until 1976, but they gave us sixteen million dollars.'

'Hang on,' I said. 'It took them fifteen *years*?'

'That's a short time, as these things go.' He stared out at the landscape. 'So many people were taken from our home in Florida to this place. This strange place. But my point is: sixteen million dollars.'

I saw what he was getting at. 'You think *that* sudden influx of money is somehow connected to this Talmascy character and his loose affiliation with certain business interests in New York.'

'You call it a loose affiliation?'

'If it had been tight,' I assured him, 'I would have gotten information at LaBracca, or at the mini golf place. My guys don't have any allegiance to Talmascy. In fact, I get the impression they wouldn't mind if I got a hold of the guy permanently.'

'Oh.' He sat back a little. 'Good.'

'So, when are you going to tell me about Eddie Harjo?'

John Horse smiled. 'He's a good guy. Do you know about the code talkers in the American World Wars?'

I gave him a nod. 'Navajo guys. All they did was speak Navajo to each other, but it was a code the Nazis couldn't break. Great trick.'

He laughed a little ruefully.

'This so-called "code talking" was invented by the Cherokee and the Choctaw during your World War One.'

'It wasn't *my* World War One.'

'But the Seminole languages were the best,' he went on. 'And Edmond Andrew Harjo was the best of them all. He was at the Normandy landing. He was at Iwo Jima.'

'And he lives here. On the Seminole land in Oklahoma.'

'He'd be about sixty now,' John Horse said. 'Why do you think you were given his name?'

'He's obviously got something to do with the missing women,' I said, 'or knows about it. Or knows Talmascy.'

'Maybe.' I could tell by the way he said it that he knew more.

'Listen,' I told him, 'I've been working overtime trying not to think about why these women have been stolen. What's happening to the mother of those two kids? And speaking of that: I been losing sleep over *those two kids*.'

'I sent them to you for just that reason,' John Horse said

softly, 'but I can see it was a little too much. I forget that you can get attached to your work. It means more to you than – well, than just *work*.'

'Like I said,' I told him, 'I'm trying *not* to think about it. I'm trying to follow this certain weird trail that will get me the kids' mother back, see? Focus on the road.'

'Always a good choice,' he said. 'Up there, at that intersection, take a left.'

I don't know what I'd been expecting, but Eddie Harjo lived in a well-kept doublewide trailer on a nice piece of farmland. Horses, goats, lots of chickens – what, to me, was a huge garden to one side. There was a rusty old Ford pickup in front, and when we pulled up past the white fence, the sun slanted just right to make it look like God was pointing right at the front door. Nice special effect.

Before we were out of the car, an older man appeared on the redwood deck front porch, shotgun in hand, down to one side.

John Horse told me, 'Just sit tight for a moment.'

And then he got out of the car.

He held up both hands, but it looked more like a greeting, not a surrender.

Harjo's face changed instantly: all smiles, and much younger looking.

'Is that the grandfather of John Horse I see?' he called out. 'Or what old man is it?'

'Look who's talking,' John Horse said, hands still up. 'You got a turkey neck!'

Harjo leaned his gun against the side of his trailer. 'It's good to see you.'

Hands down, John Horse took a few steps closer to the man. 'I'm very happy that you're still alive.'

'Why wouldn't I be alive?' Harjo asked. 'Nothing can kill me. I lived inside the White Man's war for five years, and even they couldn't kill me!'

John Horse motioned for me, and I eased out of the car.

'This is my friend, Foggy Moscowitz,' he told Harjo. 'He's helping me. You've heard of Topalargee, from where I live in Florida.'

Harjo nodded, but his eyes were on me, all suspicion.

'Her mother is missing,' John Horse went on. 'Along with other Seminole women from Florida. He's helping me to find them, and he's taking good care of Topalargee and her brother.'

'All right,' Harjo said slowly.

'You know something,' John Horse said and waited.

There was a nice breeze, and it stirred up the corn in the garden patch beside the trailer. It was a tough moment for me, because farming and crops and chickens – it was all a mystery. I think I was a little overwhelmed by . . . I don't know. Nature.

'What is it that you think I know?' Harjo said after a while.

'You know Bear Talmascy,' I said.

Maybe I shouldn't have said it right out like that. Maybe I ought to have waited for John Horse. But, as I mentioned, I was not exactly in my element. Outdoors, the bright sunshine, the smell of hay: it was confusing.

Harjo stood frozen for a moment, and then he spat over the side of his porch.

'Is that a response to Talmascy?' I asked. 'Or me?'

'He's an owl creature,' Harjo whispered. 'Night demon.'

'So, you know him,' I said casually. 'He's been stealing women from my current home town, Fry's Bay. And one of them is the mother of some children I'm supposed to help. So, if you could just tell me how to find this guy, Talmascy, I'll go beat him up or kill him or something. Then I can take the women back to Florida where they belong. Cool?'

'He's very direct,' Harjo said to John Horse.

'He's a Jew.'

To John Horse that seemed like an explanation.

Harjo raised his eyebrows and smiled at me. 'Brother! Why didn't you tell me?'

I glanced at John Horse before I said, 'Well, you know, sometimes it's not to my advantage just to blurt it out like that.'

'I know,' Harjo commiserated. 'I was in the big war all about that sort of thing. A lot of Jews in prison.'

'A lot of Jews dead,' I said. 'Difficult to talk about.'

'I understand. Sorry.'

'About Talmascy,' John Horse interceded.

'Sure.' Harjo nodded and picked up his gun. 'You can come in.'

'Isn't this Belinda's place?' John Horse asked.

'She won't mind.' And Harjo disappeared inside.

John Horse headed toward the door without looking at me. I followed.

The inside of the place was as Spartan as John Horse's cinderblock castle in the Florida swamp. No pictures on the walls, no bric-a-brac. The living room, if that's what you called it, had a single ratty armchair and a couple of ladder backs, all facing an ancient blond-wood television set.

'Does that thing work?' I asked him, pointing at it.

He nodded. 'All three channels! I like "M.A.S.H."'

I didn't know what that was, but I nodded like I did. I didn't own a television. That, plus the fact that I didn't know the difference between football and pinochle, made it impossible for me to have any sort of small talk with half the population of America.

Harjo took a seat in the armchair and nodded in the direction of the other chairs in the room.

I sat. John Horse did not.

'Bear Talmascy is lost,' Harjo began. 'He isn't a human being any more. His spirit is gone from his body, I think. I don't know what he is now. He was always hanging out in Oklahoma City, trying to get on the inside of Pody Poe's gambling operation, but he was small potatoes until recently. Suddenly he's got money and a little bit of reputation. I don't know why, but I can tell you that the criminals in Oklahoma City don't like him, and no self-respecting Seminole will speak to him. He pays some of us off, but the rest, we turn away from him.'

'Why?' I asked.

'You already know,' he said softly. 'He brings women here against their will. Seminole women. They're kept where we never see them, in a couple of houses just outside of Tecumseh.'

'About halfway between here and Oklahoma City,' John Horse piped in.

'What for?' I pressed. 'Why does he bring these women here?'

Harjo shrugged. But I could see in his eyes he had ideas, and they weren't very good ones.

'OK, let me venture a wild idea that I've been forming for a while now,' I said. 'The Seminole Nation of Oklahoma gets federal money based on population, right? I know this because of – well, a previous case.'

Harjo nodded slowly.

'So, Talmascy figured out a way to make money by counting these extra people, these women, as members of the Oklahoma congregation. Something like that. It's a variation of a tried and true Social Security scam. Get the extra money based on population, only take the money for yourself. The thing is it looks a lot more legal because they've got proof: there actually are more people there – these Florida Seminoles.'

Harjo sat forward. John Horse was frozen, waiting for me to go on with my raving.

'But once these women are here,' I went on, 'you don't see them, you said. They're kept apart. And the choices start getting pretty terrible after that.'

'Prostitution,' John Horse said.

'Judging from the way Sharp and Duck behave,' I said, 'does it seem likely that their mother would cotton on to that?'

John Horse shook his head. 'Not unless she was drugged. I've heard of that.'

Harjo nodded sagely. 'I saw that on "Kojack". Twice.'

'Well,' I hedged, 'I don't know if you'd consider this worse, or not, but a part of the Social Security scam I was talking about includes, like, *disposing* of certain people in order to collect their checks for a while. I mean, it's only a couple of hundred bucks per person, but if you have even, say, ten people, two thousand dollars a month buys a guy a lot of nice suits.'

'Talmascy would do that,' Harjo agreed. 'I told you: his spirit was gone from his body.'

'Maybe he came up with this idea,' I concluded, 'and got Poe to bankroll him – you know, transportation expenses and whatever.'

'With the help of your New York friends?' John Horse asked.

'Not my friends,' I told him. 'But yes. And now Talmascy is in the process of collecting the money and paying Poe off.'

'It's possible.' Harjo stood up.

I stood too. 'So, let's go to this place, these houses you just told me about, and get our people. Simple.'

John Horse didn't move. 'I don't think it will be that simple.'

I understood what he meant. 'He'll have guys. Sure.'

'Maybe even more owl people,' John Horse said. 'They're not so easy to beat.'

I didn't want to offend anybody by calling their superstitions ridiculous, but I couldn't help myself.

'I understand that this "owl people" thing is a story to scare children,' I began to John Horse.

'*They* believe it,' he interrupted.

'They drink human blood,' Harjo chimed in. 'And they eat human organs. I've seen them do it.'

I started to try again. 'Look . . .'

But John Horse held up a single finger.

'Even if they do it *just* to scare other people,' he said to me, 'is that really the sort of person you want to walk up to and say, "Give me the women, I'm taking them back to Florida"?'

'You make a point,' I admitted. 'At the very least, they'll have guns.'

'You don't have a gun?' Harjo asked me.

'He doesn't like them,' John Horse explained.

'That's not what all Jews think,' Harjo said. 'The guys I fought with in the war—'

'In my experience,' I interrupted, 'there *is* no such thing as "what all Jews think". If you get three Jews together in a locked room, they'll come out with four different opinions on any subject. I just don't like guns. They go off. And when they do, somebody's liable to get hurt, and sometimes it might be me.'

'He's *used* guns before,' John Horse went on. 'And he's pretty good at it. He probably even has one on him right now. He just doesn't like them.'

Harjo shrugged. 'I have a shotgun.'

I bit my lip. 'Against my entire upbringing, I am forced to ask: should we call the cops?'

They didn't like that idea any more than I did.

'No telling which cops are a part of it,' John Horse said.
'Like the ones in Fry's Bay.'

I nodded.

'So Talmascy's got guys there at these houses,' I ventured.
'Should we have guys? Do you have any idea where we might get guys of our own?'

'Oh.' Harjo looked out one of the windows. 'Sure. When I tell the neighbors what's going on, we'll probably only get a couple hundred volunteers.'

FIFTEEN

Tecumseh, Oklahoma, was named after a leader of the Shawnee. He had a war named after him, against the United States, aligning him and the Shawnee with the British in the War of 1812. The Shawnee were originally from around the Ohio River, but sometime in the early 1800s, a lot of them came to what was called the 'Indian Territory' now referred to as Oklahoma.

One of Tecumseh's main beefs with the government, as I had heard it, was that he considered all so-called 'Indian' land to be owned in common by all tribes. But he also had a brother known as The Prophet. His given name was *Lalawethika*, which means 'He Makes a Loud Noise'. His noise was that white people were all children of the Evil Spirit and all the tribes in the Midwest ought to fight them, but that went to hell when Tecumseh was killed.

The town itself wasn't very noisy at all. It had been a cotton town until the Depression. After that, the population dropped and it was a pretty sleepy burg, under five thousand people. And the outskirts were a lot of flat land; dry dust.

The group of houses where Harjo thought the women were kept would have given the word *shack* a bad name. Three of them, each one worse than the other. That crappy asbestos shingling, pale green, all falling down and rotting wood. About eight hundred square feet apiece. Windows boarded up. The front doors had padlocks on them.

And there were men with guns wandering around, looking mean and hot and hungry. About ten of them.

The sky was high and pale blue, no clouds, too much sun, when my black T-Bird pulled up a little too close to the first house. Behind me there was a caravan of at least thirty other vehicles, mostly pickups. Every one of them had at least two guys inside. And I use the term 'guys' generically, as nearly half were women. Pissed-off, steely-eyed Seminole women. With very big guns.

As they drew closer, these cars and trucks gathered by Eddie Harjo, they formed a circle around the three houses, pointed in, headlights on, engines roaring.

The guards, the Caucasian men who were supposed to be guarding the three houses, turned even whiter than they ordinarily were. Guns up, hands shaking, eyes wide and bloodshot.

I stepped out of the car, along with John Horse, and smiled at one of the guards.

'I don't like your chances here,' I said to him. 'Just put your guns down and walk away.'

'You–you're trespassing,' he managed to say. 'Private property.'

He aimed his gun at me.

'You don't really have much of a choice,' I told him sympathetically. 'You're, like, surrounded.'

Then John Horse called out a single word, and every car and truck door opened. Out came Seminole men and women, guns pointed, glaring. Silent as the grave.

'I've never really been a part of anything like this,' I said a little louder. 'And I have to tell you, it feels pretty cool.'

'Trespassing!' the guard repeated in a very shaky voice.

'Look,' I went on. 'I don't want to tell you your business, but you're Custer, and this guy with me is Crazy Horse.'

John Horse waved at them amiably.

It was immediately clear that the guard didn't know what I meant, so that told me how stupid he was.

'This land is protected by Bear Talmascy,' he said, trying to sound a little bolder, 'and he's a big deal in these parts.'

John Horse stared at the guy and called out another word, a single syllable.

Every Seminole gun made a cocking noise. I started sweating from the sound of it, and the guns weren't even aimed at me.

About half the guards lowered their guns right away. One of them even put his rifle down on the ground.

'You can walk away from here now, like Foggy said,' John Horse said softly. 'Or you can die in the dirt. I don't really care which. But one or the other is going to happen in the next sixty seconds. One . . .'

Most of the guards ditched their guns then. Two held out, including the main one we'd been talking to. He was about twenty, crew-cut jumper, dirty jeans. He was wearing a work shirt that said *Steve.*

'Seriously,' I said, taking a step toward him. 'Steve. Considering that you're guarding Seminole women, the people in these trucks that have you outgunned, they would *rather* kill you. Do you want to die? Or do you want to go into town and have a beer?'

He squinted. 'I know you?'

'No.'

'How you know my name?'

That made John Horse laugh.

I called out to the rest of the white guys, 'If you've already set your guns down, cop a walk, it's OK. Just take off and no hard feelings.'

All but Steve and one other guy split. Jumped into pickups of their own, and evaporated like the sweat on Steve's forehead was trying to do.

Steve kept his rifle pointed at me. It was a hunting rifle, well-used, and he had the look in his eye, the one that said he'd killed more than animals with it.

'I'd rather you didn't shoot me, Steve,' I told him. 'I've got a mother and an aunt in Brooklyn, and two little kids in Florida counting on me. And it won't accomplish anything. The second you fire, you'll be a whole lot dead.'

'Mr Talmascy already paid me a *lot* of money.' But I could tell his resolve was weakening.

'Right,' I said. 'Then why don't you go and spend some of it instead of getting dead?'

That made him think.

'Bear Talmascy is already dead,' John Horse said calmly. 'His body just doesn't know it yet.'

That scared Steve – you could tell by his eyes.

'Go on, Steve,' I encouraged him. 'Walk away. Live to do something stupid another day, right?'

Steve surveyed the fifty or sixty people surrounding him

with guns. He was slow; it apparently took a lot of his brain power to think it all out but, in the end, he lowered his rifle. 'Come on, little brother,' he said to the only other remaining idiot. 'Let's go get us a damn Arby's.'

With that, they both turned and got into the last truck, a cherry-red Ford, jacked up, with oversized tires. They made a show of roaring off, spewing dust.

Everything was quiet for a minute, and then Eddie Harjo called out a couple of words I didn't know, and most of the people got back in their trucks and split.

A few pulled up near us while John Horse and I went to the closest house.

John Horse had a small crowbar that Harjo had given him. He snapped the padlock off the door in three seconds.

I opened it up, but nothing happened. He said a couple of other words I'd never heard, and a dozen women swept toward him from the darkened rooms.

'Echu Matta?' I called out. 'I've come here because your children are looking for you.'

Nothing.

John Horse asked a few of the women about the kids' mother as they went past him out into the sunlight and the waiting arms of caring strangers.

No one knew a thing.

'One of the other houses,' John Horse said to me.

In the second house, we found nine women from John Horse's village. They were all very happy to see him, but not like Caucasian happy – nothing effusive or loud. Still, I noticed that just seeing him immediately erased a whole lot of worry lines in their faces. Their clothes were a little worse for wear, and they were very thirsty. The locals gave them all a good bit of water. I didn't like what that said about their treatment.

But still no Echu Matta.

After a little reassurance from John Horse that I was on the level, one of the women volunteered that she'd worked at the Benton with the kids' mother.

'Echu Matta,' she said, her voice almost a whisper, 'might be dead. She bit a man's ear off and broke his arm. She was fierce when they put us in the shipping container in Fry's Bay. They put the rest of us in and locked the door, but they took her away.'

'And since you got here,' I said, 'you haven't heard anything about her?'

She shook her head. 'John Horse says you're helping her children.'

'I'm trying.'

'What are you helping them to do?'

'Yeah,' I said, looking around the complex, 'I'm helping them find their mother.'

'Oh,' she said. 'Well. If she's not dead, Bear Talmascy might know where she is. If she is dead, of course, he wouldn't know anything about her, because he's lost his ability to see the afterlife.'

'How do you know that name?' I asked. 'He's from Oklahoma. John Horse always tells me that the Oklahoma Seminoles and the Florida families don't really know each other. Did you see him in Fry's Bay? Do you know him?'

'No, I don't know him,' she said. 'I just heard Echu Matta yelling about him as they were taking her away, in the abandoned bakery.'

'How did *she* know his name?' I asked her.

She looked back and forth between me and John Horse a couple of times before she spoke.

'*Ehee,*' she said.

'What's that word?' I asked John Horse. 'What does that mean?'

He sighed, and tried to avoid eye contact with me.

'What is it?' I asked him. 'What's the problem?'

'It's one of our words for *husband*,' he said. 'I probably should have told you about that.'

SIXTEEN

A couple of hours later, I stood in the Oklahoma City Greyhound bus station with John Horse. He was wearing a T-shirt that said 'Museum of Osteology: Make no Bones About It!' The museum, I learned, had more than five thousand animal skeletons from all over the world. It was the only museum of its kind in the world. And it was located in Oklahoma City. John Horse thought the shirt was funny. He thought it would lighten the mood.

'I hope you understand,' he told me. 'I have to go back home with these women. Just like you have to stay here and find Bear Talmascy. And Echu Matta.'

'It's a long ride.' I stared at the greyhound on the side of the bus.

'It'll be nice to stretch out. Your car is very cramped.' He smiled.

I looked down. 'Am I sure I'm doing the right thing?'

'Are you ever?'

'No.' I shrugged. 'But I guess I always know when I'm going wrong. And I'm not wrong to be here in Oklahoma. She's here, I can feel that. The kids' mother is somewhere in this city.'

'With Bear.' He nodded.

We'd already discussed how it wouldn't have mattered if I'd known that Bear was the kids' father. He was so estranged that the kids wouldn't have known who he was. Still, John Horse felt bad about not telling me that particular family secret, especially as Echu Matta had insisted that nobody outside the family should know it.

The bus was ready to leave, and neither one of us was very good at saying goodbye. He tilted his head. I raised my eyebrows. That was about it. He got on the bus, and the bus pulled out of the station.

At that moment, I felt more out of place than I ever had in

my life. Fish out of water. Oklahoma City seemed so dry and hot, and I was sure I was the only Jew within a hundred miles.

Maybe it was just because of John Horse's T-shirt, but it felt like a city of bones, the skeleton's home place. Dust to dust.

In that cheery frame of mind, I headed back to the Hook 'N' Slice to see if I could get a bead on Pody Poe. Who would, in turn, direct me to Bear Talmascy. I knew it was risky, but I really didn't want to stand around the bus station thinking too much.

As I parked my car at the putt-putt course, I was weirdly relieved to see that Rita was still at the counter, talking on the phone.

And when I approached, Rita gave me the eye and said, 'Sorry, I'll call you right back. Visiting fireman alert.'

I got myself into the shade of the booth's roof and leaned in a little.

'Look who came back,' Rita said, all sultry.

'Yeah,' I said, 'I'm happy to see you too, but I'm also in a little trouble. I just busted a whole bunch of women out of some houses that I think Mr Poe owns, see? And those women are on a Greyhound headed for Florida. Mr Poe might be a little ticked off.'

Rita was wise. 'You mean the Indians.'

'Seminole women, yes.'

'Well.' Rita looked around. 'You didn't hear it from me, but Mr Poe was none too happy about that whole deal. I hear he complained about it to New York. They didn't like it either. It was strictly for the money, you understand.'

'I do understand about the money. That's why I'm worried. I don't want to get dead from doing the right thing.'

'Liberating the Indians was the right thing,' Rita agreed. 'So, you didn't come back to see me, you came back to get next to Mr Poe.'

'Why couldn't it be both?' I asked. 'Just because I'm not walking on the wild side, that doesn't mean I don't need a drink.'

'You have no idea how good a gin and tonic tastes after

sitting in this stupid booth all day,' Rita told me, then leaned closer. 'And just a *little* bit of weed.'

'But where can a nice Jewish man and a boy named Rita go, of an afternoon, for such delights?' I wanted to know. Rita grinned like the sun. 'I have just the spot. It's where Mr Poe has a bit of an afternoon snack himself.'

'Lovely Rita,' I announced, 'I am now officially a member of your fan club.'

'You *know* that's where I took my name,' Rita said. 'From that old Beatles song, "Lovely Rita, Meter Maid".'

'It occurred to me,' I said.

'And I get to ride in that swanky black Porsche of yours.'

I shook my head. 'You kids today. That is a 1957 Thunderbird, pal. Coolest American-made car in the world.'

'*Je m'excuse, mon amour*,' Rita intoned. 'Will you still let me ride?'

'*Bien sûr, ma petite.*' My accent wasn't as good as Rita's, but I got points for trying, I could tell.

Half an hour later we were sailing down East First Street toward a rundown section of Bricktown. So-called, Rita explained to me, because of all the old brick buildings there. We were headed for an establishment that didn't have a name, but Rita called it a 'moral-free zone'. An oasis of gilded fun in an otherwise drab and judgmental city.

Turned out to be a scary-looking warehouse district, a place where I was almost certain my car would be hassled.

'You have to understand,' I explained to Rita as we pulled up to the curb close to a red door, 'that this car is my last connection with my home in New York. I can't have anything happen to it, like getting boosted, for example.'

Rita laughed. It was like flute music.

'Your car is safer here than in a bank vault, chum. *Nobody* messes with Pody Poe, and this is one of his secret hangouts. One that everybody knows about.'

With that, Rita hopped out of the car and zipped to the red door.

'Let me go in first,' she said. 'They don't like to see a stranger's face just pop in, right?'

I nodded.

Rita opened the door, surveyed, waved to someone and then motioned me in.

Considering the condition of the building on the outside, the place was a big surprise on the inside. I don't know what I was expecting, but what I walked into was a high-end New York bar, like the 21 Club or something. It was quiet, calm, elegant. Maybe five or six guys I could see sipping martinis and talking quietly.

Rita was out of place, but nobody gave a second look.

I got about five feet into the place and the only guy at the bar twirled on the stool and let out a breath.

'You gotta be Foggy Moscowitz,' he said in a big, booming voice. 'New York told me you were coming.'

Like 'New York' was the name of a guy he went to grammar school with.

'And you must be Mr Poe,' I said, using the tone of deference I had learned from a lifetime of dealing with connected guys. 'I apologize for bothering you. I have a problem and I hope you can help me. I ask with respect.'

He nodded sagely. 'Bear Talmascy and his estranged wife.'

Rita winked at me. 'I'm going to the bar. Care for a drink?'

I shook my head, eyes still on Poe.

Rita sauntered over and sat at the far end of the bar so as not to appear too curious about the rest of my conversation with Poe.

Poe looked over his shoulder at Rita for a second, then back at me.

'Good kid,' he said about Rita. 'Don't know which end is up, but I was a little wild at that age too. Weren't we all?'

I nodded.

'So,' he went on, 'you'd like to find Bear's wife.'

'I work for Child Protective Services in Florida,' I began.

He held up his hand. 'Please do not give me your life story. I already know it. You stole cars, you feel guilty, you're making amends in Florida. You're a regular hoodlum Robin Hood. You don't care about Bear or what he does, you just want to get the mother and child reunion. You know that song?'

I didn't.

'Paul Simon,' he said, like I was an idiot. 'I figured you know it. He's a Jew. Paul Simon is.'

I nodded, even though I didn't know who Paul Simon was.

'OK, well, anyway.' Poe sighed. 'I wasn't crazy about Bear's scheme to begin with. And that's when I thought he was just going to con these women into moving to Oklahoma with some sort of scheme. I didn't know he was gonna, like, *kidnap* anybody. Jeez.'

'Why was it just women, do you know?' I wondered.

'I didn't ask,' he said. 'I assume his intention was to sell them, or turn them.'

I assumed that the phrase 'turn them' had something to do with prostitution. I mean, he wasn't going to turn them into ballerinas.

'Well,' I said, 'you are correct that I'm primarily interested in Talmascy's wife, which I didn't know she was until I got to Oklahoma. Her children need her, and I am responsible for her children. So.'

Poe grimaced; it was a horrible expression. I didn't know whether he was trying to smile or threaten me.

'You say you are primarily interested in this one woman,' he told me, his voice softer than before. 'And yet you have liberated all the women Bear brought to Oklahoma. I understand that they're already on their way back to Florida.'

'News travels fast.' I kept a steady eye on him.

'Your problem is one of economics,' he said simply. 'Unsavory as Mr Talmascy's endeavor may have been, I gave him money to do it. Money which he was going to give back to me, only double. He has not made all the payments. If he has no wherewithal to do that, then I am out a considerable stack of green.'

'I see the problem,' I agreed. 'Hand me a number and I will see if I can match it.'

'You will give me double what I gave him?'

I nodded.

'And of course you realize that this is all tied up with New York,' he went on, 'so you can't really call on those guys for help. It's robbing Peter to pay Paul, you understand.'

'I believe that I can work something out, yes. I will make a call as soon as I leave here.'

'Well,' he said, and he sounded genuinely relieved. 'Then you have my blessing. As I said, I was not too crazy about this business ever.'

'You would like your money before you tell me where Bear and his wife might be.'

'No, please! I know you're a man of your word!' He was sincerely agitated. 'I trust you implicitly. If you say you'll get me the moolah, you'll get me the moolah.'

'And you know where I live,' I added.

'And I know where you live,' he repeated.

I gave him my calmest face, but inside my brain there was a major uproar. I thought of six different ways to get money to give to Pody Poe. And I rejected every single one of them. Still, I couldn't resist the buy-now-pay-later proposition.

'Right, then,' I said. 'Just tell me the sum you have in mind, and the address where I can find the happy couple.'

'Rita,' he called out.

That's all. Rita reached behind the bar and got out a pencil and a notepad; jotted something down while downing what looked like a frozen daiquiri. Then Rita moved to my side in a flash and handed me the notepad – the whole thing.

On the top page was a dollar sign followed by fewer numbers than I expected, and an address that didn't seem too complicated.

Rita was, once again, more than met the eye: knew exactly what to write down instantly.

'Want me to go with you to find this place?' Rita asked me softly.

'No, thanks,' I said. 'I'll find it.'

Rita shrugged and leaned close to me.

'PS,' Rita whispered, 'Mr Poe doesn't own those houses where the women were.'

Then Rita returned to the bar.

'Those aren't your houses where the women were being kept?' I said out loud before I could think better of it.

Poe's face only flickered for a second. 'Family name of Wilkins. Associates. They own the houses. Supposed to be for people who work their oil fields.'

From the sound of his voice, they were associates he didn't care for.

'Right,' I told him, backing away. 'Thanks very much for everything, Mr Poe.'

'Want some guys to come with you?' Poe called out. 'Bear's a pretty big guy.'

'Thanks,' I said. 'I'll be all right.'

'You sure?' Poe said. 'I don't get my money if you get dead.'

'I'm not really in the mood to die in Oklahoma,' I told him.

'I guess you know what you're doing,' he said.

'Not even a little bit,' I assured him as I backed out the door.

SEVENTEEN

As I got in my car, I wondered why I hadn't asked for directions, or taken Rita up on the offer to ride along. Was it that I didn't want to look confused in front of Pody Poe? Or was it the 'fish out of water' feeling that put me out of whack? Or maybe it even had something to do with the latent disappointment that I hadn't found the kids' mother in one of those crap houses where Talmascy kept the women.

Oklahoma City was a very strange place for me to be.

I sat in the car for a moment, staring at the address on the paper: 1700 North Lincoln Boulevard. And then I remembered passing it on the way to Bricktown. It was just south of the capital. Nice neighborhood, big Tudor homes from the 1920s. I got my bearings and lit out.

All of a sudden, I didn't need anybody's help. I knew what was what. I had instincts.

A short drive and there I was, in what they called the Lincoln Terrace neighborhood. There were new-looking signs: *Historic Preservation District*.

The house in question was a big white number, about two thousand square feet, short yard, a couple of chimneys. A real Caucasian rich-guy crash pad.

I parked in front and reached for the glove compartment; fetched my gun. Ordinarily I would never have considered such a thing, but Poe's voice was in my head: 'Bear's a pretty big guy.'

I checked the pistol, an old Smith & Wesson .38. It was supposed to have belonged to my father when he worked for The Combination, which the press foolishly referred to as 'Murder, Inc.' I slipped it into my pants at the small of my back and got out of the T-Bird slowly.

It was still very sunny, not much breeze, zero cloud cover. And then, out of the blue, I was thinking about a movie I saw on television when I was a kid. *High Noon*. The marshal had to face the bad guys all by himself. I figured it was the western setting that had me thinking about Custer, earlier, and Gary Cooper outside Bear's house. But the feeling of being all alone was pressing down on me.

What the hell was I doing in Oklahoma? For that matter, what the hell was I doing out of Brooklyn?

A couple of thoughts rose up then that I'd tried to keep under cover. It looked like Icepick Franks had killed Pan Pan Washington, but it also looked like Icepick had dumped Pan Pan's body in my bay to send me a message. It had to be a message about Pody Poe, and Bear Talmascy, and the mother of the children I was supposed to be looking after.

Considering all of that, the web of the universe seemed particularly well put together. You know, like the kind of web that spiders use to catch poor, unsuspecting flies.

That's the mood I was in when I knocked on the door of 1700 North Lincoln Boulevard.

A man the size of a small mountain answered the door.

'Yes?'

I held out my hand. 'My name is Foggy Moscowitz, and I'm with Child Protective Services in Fry's Bay, Florida. If you're Bear Talmascy, I have a message from your children.'

It was a wild gambit. In the first place, who knew if the kids belonged to Bear? Just because he'd been married to their mother didn't mean they were his. In the second, what would keep him from pounding me into the front porch like any one of the other nails there? His fist was big enough to do it.

But instead, the big guy sighed like I'd told him his mother died.

'Yeah. I heard of you.'

He stepped away from the door. I didn't move.

'Are you Bear Talmascy or not?' I asked him.

He disappeared into the shadows of the entrance hall. That made me nervous.

A second later, his voice whispered, 'Come on in.'

I still didn't move. 'We can talk on the porch.'

'Don't you want to see Echu Matta?'

'Is she in there?' I asked, pretending to scratch an itch in the small of my back.

Without warning, his giant hand reached out from behind the door and grabbed the front of my suit coat and I was pulled into the house, nose to nose with Bear.

My .38 was out instantly, and I shoved it into his ear.

'Steady,' I said softly.

And then I cocked the pistol. Probably sounded loud next to his lobe like that.

'I just didn't want to talk on the front porch in a white neighborhood like this,' he said, like I'd hurt his feelings. 'Gee.'

He let go of my coat and I dropped back, but the gun was still touching his head.

'To answer your question: yes, I want to see Echu Matta,' I said. 'Right now.'

'Sweetheart!' he bellowed.

A woman appeared in the light at the end of the short entrance hall. She was a larger version of Sharp, the Wonder Girl. Dressed in jeans and a dirty work shirt, her face smudged or bruised, her hair like black fire. Her hands were tied in front of her with plastic handcuffs like cops used sometimes in riots. Her face was hard as stone.

'There,' Talmascy said. 'She's alive and well.'

'Except for the cuffs,' I had to say.

'Well,' he explained reasonably, 'if I took off the cuffs, she'd probably try to kill me.'

Echu Matta lifted her right ankle then, to demonstrate that she was chained to something in the next room by a long chain.

'And I guess if you took that chain off,' I said, 'she might try to get away.'

'Yeah.' He was unapologetic. 'We got issues. I just want to talk with her.'

'*Efa!*' she snarled.

I knew that one: Seminole for *dog*.

'She doesn't seem amenable to conversation,' I told him.

He shrugged. 'You know how women are.'

'I don't think we'd agree on the subject,' I said. 'Do you want to hear the message from your children or not?'

Echu Matta was suddenly still – eerily still.

'I ain't got no kids,' Bear said, his irritation growing with each word. 'We had a daughter that died in childbirth. I left Florida after that. Came home for a couple of weeks about eight years ago – wait. We did sleep together then. I had a kid? Wait.'

He turned to Echu Matta. His eyes looked the way a cow looks when it knows it's going to the slaughter house.

'If you had waited a few hours,' Echu Matta said, voice as cold as concrete, 'you'd know that our daughter came back to life. Her name is Topalargee. And after you came back and raped me eight years ago, we had a son. A son you will *never* know!'

He looked at me and his eyes were wet.

'I have children?'

I shook my head. 'No. She has children. You? You don't even have a soul.'

I scraped his ear with my gun, pointed it into the wall, and fired. The sound shattered his eardrum and his head snapped sideways. I lifted my knee then as hard and as fast as I could, twice, right between his legs. When he doubled over, I hit the back of his head with the gun, right there in the spot at the base of the medulla that was supposed to put him to sleep.

He went down, all right; he just wasn't out.

He rolled, and when he was on his back on the floor, there was a gun in his hand. He fired, but the shot was wide and cracked the ceiling.

I kicked his gun hand and then dropped on top of him, my pistol pressing on his left eyeball.

'I really don't want to shoot you in the eye,' I told him. 'But it wouldn't be the worst thing I've ever done.'

'Don't kill him!' Echu Matta cried out.

I kept my eyes on Bear.

'If you say so,' I answered. 'But I'm going to have to do something, or he'll shoot us both.'

'No,' she snapped. 'I mean I want you to drag him over here to me so that I can kill him myself!'

'Ah.' I smiled at Bear. 'You're really in Dutch with the missus now, brother.'

He nodded. 'We never really got along.'

'Well, you have two pretty great kids.'

'That's why you're here?' he asked me. 'To help my children?'

I shook my head. 'I thought I made that clear. I came to help *her* children. Echu Matta.'

'Are they all right?' she asked, clearly afraid of my answer.

'No,' I told her firmly. 'They are most definitely *not* all right. Topalargee is in the hospital because Bear almost killed her in that abandoned bakery in Fry's Bay, and the boy is by her side, afraid he's going to lose his sister *and* his mother. So, no.'

Bear's eyes swelled, a look of panic. 'That was my daughter?' he muttered. 'That *midget* with a knife?'

It only took me a second to respond.

'I don't care for the word *midget*,' I said. 'I think I *am* going to let your wife kill you.'

And I bashed the side of his head five or six times until he was unconscious.

Echu Matta sat on the sofa in the living room on Lincoln Boulevard while I told her, as briefly as I could, my story.

The conclusion was: 'So John Horse and I had to leave town in search of Bear Talmascy and you. The rest of the women are already on their way back to Florida. On a bus with John Horse.'

I took a second to look around at the room. It was nicely appointed, but like something out of a demonstrator model – no real personal touches. Contemporary furniture in cream and gold, a fake Monet over the gas-log fireplace, and wall-to-wall carpet that *almost* matched the furniture.

'You stayed behind to find me?' She stared.

'I told your kids I would find you.'

I'd never seen a Seminole woman with tears in her eyes. It was a little unnerving.

'Bear lost his spirit a long time ago.' She glanced down at his unconscious body beside the sofa.

'He's an owl person or something,' I said. 'That's what they say.'

'That is what they say,' she agreed. 'He has strange powers.'

'Maybe,' I said. 'But what good is magic if it can't protect you from, excuse my language, a swift kick in the nuts?'

That made her laugh, which made me happy.

'What are we going to do with him?' she asked me.

'Yeah,' I said, sitting back in the wing chair, 'that's a puzzle. Which cops are straight and which ones belong to Pody Poe?'

'I don't know who that is.'

'Local guy, bankrolled this particular business venture,' I explained.

'Which was what, exactly? No one ever told us what Bear was going to do with us.'

'I only have guesses, and none of them are very nice.' I took in a breath. 'I think he was trying to increase the verifiable Seminole population here in Oklahoma to get a bigger bite of the government money, like a Social Security scam, you understand?'

She nodded. 'And it would make sense to the government agents. Most of the Seminoles who were brought here originally were men.'

'Importing women would balance the population.'

'Yes.' She was glaring at Bear. 'What did he think he was going to do to make us stay here?'

'That's the unsavory part, to me,' I went on. 'I think he might have intended to sell you once you were counted by the government. He'd get money two ways: for the extra people, and then for selling you.'

'As what?' She spat out a harsh breath. 'Seminole women don't make good prostitutes or tame servants. We'd escape.'

I shifted uncomfortably in my chair. 'Not if you were drugged all the time.'

'Oh.'

Bear moaned. He was waking up.

I cocked my pistol and leaned forward, but Echu Matta was already off the sofa and on top of him.

She took hold of his ears, one in each hand, and shook his big head like it was a rag.

'I'm going to speak to you in English,' she whispered

harshly, 'because I don't want to defile the language of my people when I talk to you. You are lost, Bear, and you will wander eternity with no home and no family. No rest. No peace. Always hungry and thirsty. Always wanting. Do you hear me?'

He opened his eyes. They were the saddest eyes I had ever seen.

'I–I wanted to start over. I wanted to be a better husband.' He swallowed. 'I thought I could end my cursed path and begin another one. I was going to get the money and then come home to you. But then, when I saw you at the Benton, and you were so angry with me, I got scared. I took you. I did that. But I thought if I got you to Oklahoma and explained—'

Echu Matta shrieked a high-pitched scrap of pain like I had never heard in my life. She started banging his head into the carpet over and over again, still screeching, not taking in a breath.

Bear just looked up at her face and took it. Until he passed out.

Then she climbed off him and shook her head.

'Too many men believe that women are things,' she said, her voice rasping and harsh. 'Mostly whites, but human beings too.'

I stood up, gun still pointed at Bear.

'I don't want to make a big deal,' I said, 'but we should get to your children as quickly as we can. And I'm a little uncomfortable just leaving Bear here. It's my estimation that he'll come after you. And me, I guess.'

She sighed. 'What can we do? I hate him, but I don't really want his blood on my hands.'

'Yeah,' I agreed, 'and shooting a guy on such nice carpeting isn't exactly my style either.'

Bear groaned.

'I do have an idea, though,' I continued. 'Do you think you could manage to tie him up so he can't get loose?'

'Yes,' she said bluntly.

'Would you do the honors, then?' I asked her. 'I am going into the kitchen. I happened to see a phone in there. I need to make a phone call.'

She went immediately to the beige floor-to-ceiling curtains at the back end of the living room, and I went into the kitchen to make my call.

In ten minutes, the curtain cords were around Bear's wrists and ankles, both behind his back, so tight that his skin was bleeding. And his back was arched in a way that made my spine ache just to look at it.

Echu Matta stood back to admire her work. 'What now?'

'Now,' I answered her, pocketing my gun, 'we go to a bar in Bricktown and hope that Pody Poe is still there.'

The unnamed bar in Bricktown was nearly deserted when the doorman let me in. Rita was at the far end of the bar, watching but not acknowledging.

Poe was sitting at a table near the front. Two guys stood behind him, one on either side. Poe had changed into golfing attire: a yellow shirt and white pants, and those stupid shoes with cleats, like golf was an actual athletic endeavor.

The place seemed moodier, but maybe it was the lighting. Less like the 21 Club; more like the waiting room at a mortuary. And just as quiet.

I stood about ten feet away from Poe's table, hands clasped in front of me. Poe was nodding like I'd said something, even though I hadn't uttered a peep since I walked in the joint.

Finally, he said, very slowly, 'I have called New York. I have spoken with people. You did not ask them for the money. The money you promised me.'

I let go a breath. 'You and I agreed that I wasn't going to ask anyone in New York for the money.'

'I *know*,' he snapped. 'But I thought you'd ask *somebody*!'

'I did ask somebody.' I tried to make my voice as soothing as possible.

'And?' he demanded.

'You want to know where I'm getting the money if it's not coming from New York?'

'I do.' His voice was getting higher.

I nodded. 'Well, I'm afraid I can't tell you that. But I can say that I've made my call, and it's a done deal. The amount you wrote on the piece of paper is on its way to you now, Western Union service. A cashier's check hand-delivered to the Hook 'N' Slice.'

'In my name?' he growled.

'Not unless your first name is *Cash*.' I glanced down toward the end of the bar. 'I told them that Rita would sign for it.'

Rita downed what was left of a daiquiri then stood, waiting.

Poe nodded, and Rita went out some back way through the kitchen without a word.

'And I thought you might like to know,' I went on, 'that Talmascy is hogtied inside that house on Lincoln Boulevard. His wife beat him up and left him that way. I thought you might want to speak with him, seeing as he has caused you no small amount of trouble. Because my guess is that when you called New York about this mess, they were unhappy with *you*. Not him. That's why you're so upset now. Not because you thought I wouldn't get your money, but because *my friends* in New York gave you what-for.'

I made quite a point of emphasizing the words *my friends*.

He wanted to say something about that, I could tell. But he didn't.

'And so,' I concluded, 'I will be leaving your city now. It's a long drive back to Florida; I want to get on the road before dark.'

'It would be a good idea,' he said carefully, 'if you didn't come back to Oklahoma City. Ever.'

'I cannot tell you how much I agree with that sentiment,' I assured him.

I suspected that I was getting off easy. I backed toward the door and dropped my arms to my side, ready to go for the pistol in my coat pocket.

But my exit was without incident.

Echu Matta was slumped down in the passenger seat of my T-Bird, sleepy in the slant of the afternoon sun. I got in and she roused herself.

'Are they going to kill Bear, the men in that place?' she asked me.

'I don't know.' I started the car. 'Let's go home – you want to?'

She smiled. I drove. In no time at all, Oklahoma City was in the rearview mirror.

EIGHTEEN

Florida

I had some very confusing feelings when I saw the sunrise over Fry's Bay. It felt like coming home. I'd never thought of Fry's Bay as home, just a place to be until I went back to Brooklyn. My *home* in Brooklyn.

Echu Matta was asleep beside me. She hadn't talked much on the trip; she said she had to get her strength and her spirit back. I understood. And to tell the truth, it was kind of nice being quiet for a while. Don't get me wrong, I loved John Horse. But sometimes he could talk too much.

The sun coming up was the color of a flamingo's wing, and the stars were still blinking up high. The ghost of a moon was haunting the western sky, and gulls were headed toward the beach. It felt like a nice ending to all the troubles.

I nudged Echu Matta.

'You want me to drive you straight to the hospital?' I asked her.

I'd been driving all night and I was bleary-eyed. She looked at me for a minute and then nodded. So straight to the hospital I went.

I wasn't sure if I should come with her into the room where her daughter was in a coma and her son was quietly freaking out. I was barely to the nurse's station when I saw the look of panic on Maggie Redhawk's face. I was suddenly afraid of what might be wrong.

'What room are they in?' Echu Matta whispered.

Maggie looked at me. 'They're gone, Foggy! Cops came and got them in the middle of the night. When I wasn't here.'

Echu Matta froze.

I was so tired I thought I'd heard wrong. 'Who's gone?' I blinked.

'I've been frantic. John Horse is nowhere to be found!'
Maggie was more emotional than I'd ever seen her.

As opposed to Echu Matta, who'd gone very still.

'Cops came and got those children out of the hospital?' I
asked slowly.

'Topalargee was awake,' Maggie told me. 'She just sat up
in bed, suddenly, when I was in there. She said you'd found
her mother, Foggy.'

That didn't surprise Echu Matta. She just nodded.

'OK.' I rubbed my face hard. 'OK. First: John Horse is
probably still on a Greyhound with the rest of the missing
women. Takes the bus twice as long to get here from
Oklahoma as it does a Thunderbird. Second: doesn't sound
like Watkins or Brady to just barge into a hospital room
and take children away. Third: when did that happen and
who was here?'

'About five hours ago,' Maggie said. 'And Betty Patten was
the nurse on duty.'

'Where's Betty now?' I asked.

'Asleep in the break room,' Maggie answered. 'I told her
not to go home.'

I smiled. 'Good. Have you spoken with your brother in the
past two days?'

Maggie shook her head. 'Why do you ask?'

'I need to see him,' I said, 'but given the current situation,
it'll have to wait. This Betty Patten's in the break room?'

Maggie pointed. Echu Matta was ahead of me.

Nurse Betty Patten was a waif. Couldn't have been more
than ninety-eight pounds, eyes like emeralds, nervous hands.
When she saw us come in, she jumped.

'Who took my children?' Echu Matta said softly.

It was more a threat than a question.

'The police came,' she said. She'd said it a dozen times
before, from the sound of her voice. Plenty of people had
already asked her what happened.

'You let them take a kid who'd been in a coma?' I asked,
just to let her know that I was familiar with the case.

'Her . . . her grandfather, the children's grandfather, said it
would be all right,' Nurse Patten squeaked.

'No,' Echu Matta said. 'Both of her grandfathers have been dead for over twenty years.'

Nurse Patten looked at me. 'They were Indians. Indian men with the police. They were the *police*.'

'Did they have any sort of paperwork?' I asked.

Nurse Patten looked away. 'No.'

'You're new here,' I said. 'I don't just mean to this hospital. You're new to Fry's Bay.'

'Uh-huh.' She nodded, still not looking at us.

'That's a midwestern accent,' I observed.

'Columbia City, Indiana.' She sighed.

'What happened?' I asked.

She finally looked over. 'Hm?'

'What happened there to make you come here? What is it you're getting away from?'

'Where are my children?' Echu Matta growled.

Which destroyed any chance of subsequent amiable conversation.

'I don't know! Are they going to fire me?' And suddenly, her face looked about ten years old.

Nurse Betty Patten was a deep well into which I chose not to dive. Her story was probably an interesting, lonely one. Like mine. But it was too much to take on, for about a million reasons.

Echu Matta turned, abruptly, and headed for the door.

'Where are you going?' I asked her, following.

'Police station.'

I fell in beside her. 'Seems like the right place. Besides, they always have coffee, and I need some.'

We were silent for the four minutes it took us to speed to the station. I went in first, kicking the door and then shoving it open so hard that it hit against the wall.

'Where are they?' I demanded before I could see if there was anybody in the room.

Jeanie's face went white.

Jeanie was a community school undergraduate student in retail management. Her job at the police department strained the concept of the part-time job. She was in the office on Tuesday mornings for an hour, and Fridays from five to seven in the evening. I had no idea what her duties were, and I always had the impression that she didn't know either.

She was alone in the office, standing beside one of three-dozen file cabinets. Her platform shoes, three-inch cork soles, only emphasized the fact that her grey miniskirt was way too short for a kid of her size. Wispy blonde hair in two side ponytails touched the shoulders of her pressed white short-sleeved blouse.

She was trying to talk, but couldn't.

'Where are my children?' Echu Matta growled low.

The sound of that voice froze my blood, and I thought that Jeanie might pass out.

'Y–your children, ma'am?' she finally managed to squeak.

'Is there anybody in holding?' I asked her. 'Anybody?'

Jeanie glanced toward the door that opened on to the cells, then back at me.

'No.' She blinked.

'Watkins and Brady?' I sighed.

'What about them?' she asked softly.

'Where are they?' I shot back.

'I don't . . . I don't know.' Jeanie lowered her voice. 'What's this about missing children?'

Echu Matta turned to me. Her face only looked half-human. 'Where are they, Foggy?' she snarled.

I squeezed my eyes shut and took in a breath. 'I don't know, and I've been driving all night. I'm not a reliable source. Come on.'

I headed for the door.

'Where are you going?' Echu Matta demanded.

'Coffee,' I answered, not looking back. 'And a donut.'

The donut shop called, appropriately enough, Donuts, was a throwback to a bygone era, right in the center of Fry's Bay. You could smell the yeast a block away. The counters were all starry Formica and the 45s in the jukebox hadn't been changed since 1957.

Cass was in charge. She was at least sixty years old, not quite five feet tall, red rouge smeared on her cheeks, red eyes set way back in her head. The henna in her hair smelled like ginger, somehow, and her face was a roadmap of the harder life elsewhere that had landed her in our little town.

When I walked in the door she growled like a dog.

'Morning, Cass,' I said, taking a stool at the bar.

'You're not supposed to be in here,' she warned me.

'I need coffee.'

Cass paused for a moment, then rolled her head and picked up the coffee pot.

Echu Matta came in then; she'd paused outside for a minute, unclear or undecided what to do. When Cass saw that face, she swallowed and stepped back three full paces.

'I don't want no trouble,' she said defensively.

'Where are the policemen?' Echu Matta whispered harshly.

'Wh–what policemen?' Cass stammered.

Then Echu Matta screamed. It was a sound filled with days of captivity, hunger, thirst, privation, pain and – most of all – rage. Not a human sound.

Cass dropped the coffee pot.

The other three people in the place froze.

I leaned forward and spoke to Cass a little meaner than I should have.

'I think you know which policemen she's looking for,' I said.

'Blake Road!' Cass said instantly. 'Blake Road. Jesus.'

I nodded. 'I'm still going to need that coffee, Cass.'

Cass didn't know what to do for a minute. Then, eyes still on Echu Matta, she backed into the kitchen.

'And a couple of crullers,' I called out.

In two shakes, Cass was back with a bagful of donuts and to-go cups of coffee.

I slapped a fiver on the counter, way more than I needed to pay. Cass had a hard enough life.

Echu Matta backed toward the door, eyes locked on Cass.

'You know to be careful with them guys, right, Foggy?' Cass said softly.

I was staring down into the bag. 'Hey!' I said. 'Eclairs!'

Echu Matta held the door open and I handed her a cup.

We headed toward Blake Road. I offered her an eclair.

'These things are so good,' I told her. 'You *have* to try one.'

She downed the hot coffee, crumpled the cup and put it in one of the pockets in her jeans. Then she reached in the bag, took out an eclair and put half of it in her mouth. I realized then that I hadn't eaten in two days, and she'd probably gone longer than that.

No wonder we were both feeling mean.

In the time it took us to walk to the abandoned building on Blake Road, Echu Matta and I had finished off a half-dozen donuts and my coffee was gone.

Even before we got to the door we could hear people talking inside. All of them were adult voices.

I put my index finger to my lips and took my pistol out. She nodded. I stood to one side of the door and she stood on the other. I crouched down and she did the same. I took hold of the handle and twisted it. Then I shoved the door in and waited.

No gunfire. That was a good sign.

I peered around the edge of the doorframe.

Brady and Watkins were staring out, flanked by three other men in very nice suits. All Seminoles.

Before I could stop her, Echu Matta was standing in the doorway grinding out some of the most vicious sounding monolog I'd ever heard. All in Seminole. All incomprehensible to me. But the meaning was clear.

So formidable was her presence that the men stood transfixed and motionless.

After a beat of silence, one of the Seminole men spoke. He said a single word.

'*Huppa.*'

Echu Matta didn't respond. But she stopped talking.

'*Huppa Iste,*' the man said louder.

'I am not a child,' Echu Matta said then. 'You don't frighten me with your supernatural inventions or your bad diction.'

I got it then. It took me a second, but the word came to me, thanks to John Horse. *Huppa* was *owl. Iste* was *person.* The guy was trying to convince her that he was some kind of spirit creature.

For some reason that irritated me beyond all measure. Probably the exhaustion and hunger.

Without thinking better of it, which I obviously should have, I stood up, muscled Echu Matta out of the doorway and shot Mr Owl Person in the shoulder. And what do you know: he screeched. Kind of like an owl. But he also bled very much like a person. I turned to Echu Matta. 'So, I guess that settles that.' Watkins had his gun out, and Brady was trying to talk. The other two Seminoles were staring at me with a mixture of vague curiosity and mild irritation, which I found strange.

'Before you guys get all excited,' I said to the room, 'this woman beside me was kidnapped, beaten, starved and otherwise inconvenienced, so I *had* to shoot *somebody*. You understand that. Also, I brought her back here from Oklahoma so that she could be reunited with her children, and now I find that someone took them. Someone who was a cop. And since I don't know any other cops in Fry's Bay as well as I know you guys, I was thinking of shooting you too. In the pursuit of my duties. See, I'm a State employee, whereas Fry's Bay cops are County. I, like, outrank you.'

No one in the room was impressed by my speech. But Echu Matta was laughing. So that was something.

Watkins was the first one to get himself together.

'I don't know how you're still alive,' he snarled, 'but you have no idea what kind of trouble you're in.'

I turned to Echu Matta. 'How do you feel about collecting everyone's gun?'

Her answer was to dart into the room immediately and begin taking weapons off the men.

Watkins started to object, but I interrupted him.

'You see that I'm in the mood to plant bullets,' I said. 'I'm very tired and I've had a bad couple of days, and I think I've got a sugar rush from donuts. I'm hopped up. So, really, I wouldn't do anything to set me off.'

'Moscowitz . . .' Brady began.

'Shut up,' I told him. 'You're first on my list.'

I wasn't sure what I meant by that, exactly, but it seemed to mean something to Brady. He shut up.

Echu Matta came back to me with an armful of guns.

'Here's what you don't know,' I announced. 'I still have

friends in New York. They pointed me to Pody Poe in Oklahoma City. That's where I found this woman. And all the other ones. They're all on a bus with John Horse, coming back to Florida. And my friends in New York are now very unhappy with Poe. Who is, in turn, very unhappy with Bear Talmascy. Who is, in turn, tied up in some upper-middle-class chateau in Oklahoma City, waiting for Poe to come and kick his head in, or some such. I tell you these things to let you know where you stand. Which is out in the cold.'

Sure, it was a little rambling, but it got the point across, I thought.

Echu Matta set all the guns down on the sidewalk in front of the vacant store. All except one. It was a sleek little Parabellum Luger Mauser, a real collector's item. She checked it like she meant business and then pointed it into the room.

'If someone doesn't tell me where my children are,' she said, cold and calm, 'I'm going to start shooting people. I'll stop when I know what I want to know.'

To prove her point, she shot one of the Seminoles. In the thigh. He sucked in a breath, gritted his teeth and said, '*Hockta*.' Then he spat on the ground.

That, of all things, got me mad.

I zoomed into the room, right up to the guy, cocked my left hand back and knocked out his two front teeth.

'You spit when you call her *woman*?' I railed. 'You didn't have a mother? You don't owe your life to a woman?'

My unfortunate ire was short-lived. The Seminole with the missing teeth knocked my gun out of my hand. The one I'd shot bopped me in the back of the head. And Watkins kicked my left shin so hard that my relatives felt it.

The next thing I knew, I was on the floor and Echu Matta fired her gun. I don't know what she fired it at, but the room went very still very quickly.

I rolled over and stared up at the men.

'You really should tell her where her children are,' I said to them, struggling to my feet. 'You probably guessed that I wasn't going to kill anybody. But she probably will, before it's all over. She could kill all five of you, in fact, and disappear into the swamp. Never seen again.'

I retrieved my gun and got to the doorway, bloodied but unbowed.

'The thing is,' she said to me once I was by her side, 'that one, the one with the missing teeth and the bullet in his thigh. He was one of the men who put us into the storage container in the abandoned bakery. He doesn't recognize me, but I know him. He's friends with Bear.'

The guy had lost some of his swagger. He was starting to feel the bullet, and his mouth was bleeding.

I smiled.

'If you'd seen what she did to Bear,' I told the guy, 'you'd need to change your pants.'

I thought that might scare him. Letting him imagine what she might have done would be a lot worse than what had actually happened.

And it worked. He began whispering feverishly to Watkins. I couldn't hear what they were saying, but it was obvious that there was concern.

Watkins sighed, nodded and looked at me. 'So, here's the deal, Foggy. We got the kids in a safe location. They're fine – at the moment. But we're going to hang on to them, see? So that you don't do something stupid. We're ready to retire, me and my friends. You let us get clear of all this, get out of town, and then we'll let you know where the kids are.'

'No good, and you know it,' I said, before Echu Matta could speak up. 'You give us the location of the children right now and we can all walk out of this building. You abscond; we retrieve.'

He understood. 'Like a race.'

'Like a bet,' I countered. 'You bet that you can disappear before I find the kids.'

'You won't come after us.' He gave me the iron stare.

'I won't. That's not my job. My job is the kids.'

He knew me well enough to know that was true.

'Right,' he said, staring me down.

But there was something else in the room. A certain odd vibe. And it was coming off Brady. He caught my eye, and I blinked. It was because of him that I wasn't dead in an alley.

Watkins would put that together, if he hadn't already. Brady wasn't who anyone thought he was.

Time to figure that out.

'The only caveat, if I may,' I told Watkins, 'is that you could give us a bogus location, and you'd be gone while we were empty-handed. So, one of you has got to stay behind. Collateral.'

'That one,' Echu Matta said, pointing her gun at the man with the missing teeth.

'It'd have more heft if we kept a cop,' I said to her.

'It won't be me,' Watkins started.

'No,' I interrupted. 'It'll be Brady. I owe him for shooting me and leaving me and John Horse to die. This is going to be fun.'

I tried to sound as mean as I could.

Brady got it. He turned to Watkins. 'No!' He sounded panicked. 'Watkins, you can't leave me with this goddam Jew!'

Watkins was not in the mood. 'You should have killed him a little better, then, Brady. Jesus.'

'Sit down, Brady,' I said, pointing my gun at him. 'I'll let you go when I have the kids, and you know I'm righteous. Sit.'

'No.'

I fired my gun. The bullet zipped by his ear. He sat down.

Watkins began his speech. 'A lot of people don't know that Blake Road was, at one time, the only access to the two-lane blacktop that came past Fry's Bay in the thirties and forties. After the highway was completed, Blake went by the wayside. But if you follow it out past the bus station – it's mostly shrubs and weeds for a while, but there's still some leftover asphalt – you'll eventually come to a big stand of pines and a couple of clapboard houses. The kids are in one of them.'

I glanced down at Brady. His eyes said that Watkins was telling the truth.

'OK,' I said.

Watkins looked at the Seminole men. 'Time to go.'

I went to Brady and Echu Matta stepped aside to let everyone pass.

When they were gone, Brady stood up. 'You can put that

gun away, Moscowitz,' he said, his southern accent completely gone.

'My guess?' I said to him, slipping my pistol back into my suit coat. 'You're FBI.'

He held out his hand. 'Special Agent Meyer Rothschild,' he said, with the hint of a smile on his lips.

NINETEEN

Special Agent Rothschild explained to us that the FBI had been wise to Bear Talmascy's scheme for a while. Bear had taken five groups of women to Oklahoma. Rothschild also told us that the FBI currently had an eye on the shack where Echu Matta's kids were being held, so we shouldn't worry.

'I'll take you to them right now,' he assured her. 'Everything's going to be fine.'

Echu Matta turned to me. 'Go home. You need sleep. I'll bring the children to you later.'

I tried to disagree, but I was truly dead on my feet.

'You should take them both to Maggie Redhawk before you do anything else,' I said. 'Your daughter's been in a coma, and your son hasn't been eating. Also, Maggie's worried.'

She nodded again. Her mind was only half with me. The other half was in a rundown shack in the woods at the other end of Blake Road.

Rothschild called for a car on some sort of government walkie-talkie he had hidden in his sock. Then he locked eyes with me.

'You realize that you and I are going to have to sit down and confer,' he said to me. 'We have lots of questions.'

'And I have lots of answers,' I assured him. 'But she's right – I'm just about useless at the moment.'

'Understood,' he said. 'How about the donut shop tomorrow morning?'

'Agreed.' And with that, I evaporated.

The front door of my apartment had never looked so good. I pulled my T-bird up as close to it as I could. I'd had better luck getting to my door drunk than I did that morning. *Dead on my feet* was an understatement.

So, when I opened my door and saw a shadowy figure sitting

in my living room, my first reaction wasn't fear or flight, it was annoyance.

'No,' I said to the shadow. 'I'm too tired to try to kill you. If you want to talk with me, make yourself comfortable and wait a couple of hours, because I'm going into my bedroom now and falling down on to my bed.'

And I headed toward the bedroom door.

But a weirdly familiar, forlorn voice stopped me in my tracks. 'Foggy?'

I turned. All the curtains were drawn, there were no lights on, no way to see his face. But the voice was impossible to miss.

I swallowed. 'Pan Pan?'

'Jesus, Foggy, you got no idea how glad I am to see you.'

I took a single step in his direction before I saw the gun in his hand.

'Is that a Luger?' I asked him.

'Oh.' He looked down at the pistol in his hand. 'Forgot I had it. I been in your apartment for two days. Sleeping on the sofa. Where you been?'

'Oklahoma.'

He nodded. 'You got the message, then.'

'Pan Pan,' I said, 'you're not dead.'

'Not quite,' he told me. 'But I been better.'

'I'm going to snap on a light now,' I said. 'And you're going to put that Luger away. OK?'

'Sounds good.' The gun vanished.

I turned on the lamp beside the sofa. And there was Pan Pan. Alive. Conservative grey suit, paisley tie, pale blue shirt. He looked like a banker. His eyes were tired but his face was calm. And his shoulders were tense, you could see that.

I sat down in my big chair.

'I'm very glad to see you,' I said. 'But I'm also confused. You've been pronounced dead in the state of Florida.'

'Really?' He leaned forward. 'What did I ever do to Florida?'

'Well,' I explained, 'Sammy "Icepick" Franks killed you and then dumped you in the bay here in the little town where I currently live.'

'They thought that was *me*?' His voice got higher.

'The stiff had your driver's license in his pocket,' I said.

'Oy.' He slouched down. 'I wondered where that was.'

'*Oy?*' I asked.

He smiled. 'I been hanging out with your mother and your aunt. *Hiding* out, actually. They're very nice.'

'Yeah,' I told him. 'I thought you'd put on a few pounds.'

That made him laugh. And there it was: the patented Pan Pan laughter. It filled up my little apartment. It banished all gloom.

'OK, let's take a step back,' I began. 'Icepick drove all the way here in that Lincoln that we sold him in order to dump a dead body in the bay. A dead body which had your identification on it.'

'That was supposed to be the message,' Pan Pan said.

'Yeah, I don't understand this use of the word *message*.'

'Right. So. The reason I was hiding out at your mother's,' he explained, 'is that all hell was breaking loose concerning some deal that Icepick didn't like but his associates in Manhattan went for anyway. Which meant that Manhattan was on edge and Icepick was on the prowl. So, guys like me, the small potatoes, scattered for cover until the storm was over.'

'Understandable.' I knew that enmity of the sort he was describing was liable to involve stray bullets. It was only prudent to take cover. And, truth be told, Pan Pan was always looking for a good excuse to hang out with my mother. 'But that still doesn't explain why you are simultaneously dead in the morgue *and* sitting in my living room.'

'Icepick told me he was going to send you a message because the deal which he didn't like involved people from here, from Fry's Bay. That's the reason he didn't like it. He knew you were here and didn't like to see you get screwed with in any way. He likes you. He must have taken my ID off me when he told me all that.'

'*Message*,' I insisted. 'You still haven't explained the term *message*.'

'Right. He said he was going to send you a message that you couldn't ignore that would explain what was going down. I just didn't know it would be a dead body that was supposed to be me. Although, you see how that would get your attention.'

'It got my attention,' I said. 'I just didn't understand what he was getting at. I'm beginning to piece it together now, but it's a little after the fact.'

'How do you mean?'

I explained, in as few words as possible, the scheme that Bear Talmascy had hatched – the kidnapping, the various fraudulent ways it would make money, and the way the women would have ended up. All of which disgusted Pan Pan.

'Now I see why Icepick was so upset,' he told me.

I shook my head.

'You never heard him talk about his mother?' Pan Pan asked. 'You talk about *your* mother like she's a saint. He doubles that times ten about his own mom. It's, like, *weird.*'

'So – what? Icepick was offended by the scheme on the basis of having a loving mother?'

'That's my thinking.'

'And he killed some poor slob and dumped his body in my bay just to alert me . . . to give me a heads up?'

Pan Pan nodded. 'Maybe it would make more sense if you knew who the stiff really was.'

'They wouldn't let me look at the body,' I said, and then my weary bones got a shock.

Pan Pan saw it happen. 'What?'

'They wouldn't let me see the body because I wasn't next of kin,' I told him, standing up. 'But they'd let you.'

'How am I next of kin to a stranger?'

I headed for the door.

'You have a much better estimation of race relations in America,' I told him, 'than the facts would support.'

'Ah,' he answered, standing up. 'Black face equals black face.'

I was out of my apartment, into my T-Bird, and off to the Coroner's Office before my poor body realized that it wasn't going to get into bed after all.

The outside observer might have wondered at my reaction to the fact that Pan Pan was not dead. But here's what I would tell that observer. My father, a guy I didn't know, was one of Red Levine's operatives in what was called The Combination, an organization that the goyishe press referred to as Murder,

Inc. Hebrew hitmen with good reputations. When my father got killed in the course of his work, Red took me under his wing. He wanted me in the organization in general, just not in the murder end of things. He started me doing this and that until I discovered my aptitude for boosting high-end autos from the swanky parts of Brooklyn. But I was still around murder every day. When you've got that much death in your daily intercourse, if I may use that word, you get a skin tougher than a tank and an attitude that some describe as *fatalistic.*

You also lose a certain ability to demonstrate your emotional content. For the most part, you lose it on purpose. It's just easier that way.

But as we were driving to the Coroner's Office, I did manage to say to Pan Pan, 'I'm glad you're not dead.'

'Oh.' He stared at the side of my face as I drove for a minute and said, 'Me too.'

'We'll sort everything out about Icepick as soon as we find out who *is* dead.'

He nodded. 'Right.'

And that was that.

Ten minutes later we pulled up to the dingy little government building near the highway that housed, among other things, the Coroner's Office. One story, all brick, dirty windows and glass doors in the front that made an awful screeching noise when you opened them.

We were almost to the office when Pan Pan said, 'Do you think it's somebody we know, this stiff?'

'I'm still trying to figure how this is a *message* from Icepick,' I told him.

'You know the man,' Pan Pan offered. 'His brain works a certain way, and that's that.'

'You mean he's not like normal people.'

Pan Pan stopped in the hallway. 'No. You and me, *we're* not normal people. Icepick is something else altogether.'

'He shot a dog.'

'There you go.' And with that, Pan Pan resumed walking.

I knew the coroner slightly, a weathered and weary civil servant by the name of Parker. Jowly, rum-eyed, fifty pounds overweight. His white lab coat always had yellow and brown stains on it, but his penny loafers were always clean.

When I opened the door and he saw me standing there, he started shaking his head. 'No, Mr Moscowitz,' he croaked. 'Them cops both told me you ain't to look at that dead body.'

The office was small: a desk, a chair, a picture of Nixon. And one wall was entirely occupied by three large chrome drawers, refrigerated, in which he could store the corpses. The door to his examination lab, in another room, was just behind his desk.

I stepped aside to reveal Pan Pan.

'I have brought the next of kin,' I explained, 'which the cops told me would be someone who *could* see the body.'

He stared for a minute, then said to Pan Pan, 'And just who might you be?'

'I am Albertus T. Washington,' he announced grandly, which was true; it was Pan Pan's given moniker.

Parker considered protesting, sniffed, gave up and ambled toward one of the chrome drawers, which he pulled open.

Pan Pan took a breath and went to look.

He stared for what seemed like a long time, then glanced my way.

'Poor Pan Pan,' he said. 'Come have a look, Foggy.'

I looked at Parker. He shrugged. I went to have a look.

The face I was staring at, only a little damaged by saltwater and several days too long above ground, was not familiar. But he was what they called a Black Seminole. These were guys who had mostly descended from runaway slaves who had made it to Florida and ended up marrying Seminole women. They were, for the most part, a tribe apart, living separate lives from other Seminoles but loosely affiliated with all of them. This gent was wearing a suit from Manny's; I would recognize one from a mile off. Manny was tailor to the criminal element in my former associates in Brooklyn and, to a lesser extent, Manhattan. Manny was as adept at making a suit as any other haberdasher in the city, but he excelled in designs that took holsters and guns into account. You could be wearing a tommy gun under one of Manny's suits and nobody would know it. In that arena, he was a magician. And this Black Seminole was wearing one of his numbers.

'Nice suit,' I said, mostly to point it out to Pan Pan.

'I noticed that,' he assured me.

'Poor Pan Pan,' I repeated, staring down.

'I will collect his effects now,' Pan Pan declared officiously.

'Sure.' Parker didn't care. One black guy's stuff didn't mean anything to him. Give it to another black guy and have done with it. 'You made funeral arrangements?'

'We're having the body shipped back home,' Pan Pan said, maintaining his air of dignity. 'We want him to be buried in a kosher graveyard.'

Which took me by surprise, and I cracked up. I laughed a little too much, but I recovered quickly.

'Grief does strange things to a person,' I explained to Parker. 'Pan Pan, he's my best friend, you understand.'

Parker was rummaging in some bin for Pan Pan's wallet.

'Takes all kinds.' He sighed.

He found what he was looking for and handed it to Pan Pan.

'That's it?' he asked Parker. 'Where's his watch? His ring?'

'No watch,' said Parker. 'No ring. Maybe the killer took them.'

'Yes. Possibly.' Pan Pan made it sound like he knew Parker had taken them.

It was a good trick. It put Parker on the defensive.

'You can have a look at the paperwork,' Parker snapped.

'I can assure you that Mr Moscowitz, here, will be investigating!' Pan Pan railed. And then he spun round and stormed out the door.

I turned to Parker. 'Sorry. Like I said: grief makes you say and do odd things.'

'Don't I know it.' He sighed again.

'OK.' And I was out the door.

Once Pan Pan and I were in the car, the first question was obvious.

'Who the hell was that guy?' he asked.

'Right,' I agreed. 'And why did Icepick kill him?'

'And then why did Icepick subsequently bring him to your hometown,' Pan Pan continued, 'and then dump him in your bay? What exactly was the message?'

'All questions that must be answered,' I concluded.

We drove the rest of the way back to my apartment in contemplative silence.

But when we pulled up close to my front door, there was Echu Matta and the redoubtable Agent Rothschild, clearly in a dither.

Before I even shut the engine off, Echu Matta was at the driver's door.

'They weren't there!' she exploded.

Rothschild was right behind her. 'They're gone.'

'Someone took them!' Echu Matta.

'Hang on.' I turned off the engine, got out of my car and turned to Rothschild. 'Your FBI guys didn't see anything?'

He started to talk but Echu Matta interrupted him.

'Someone took them, Foggy!' Echu Matta railed.

'Is it possible,' I said calmly, 'that the kids escaped the shack where the cops were keeping them?'

They both began to talk at the same time. I held up my hand.

'Steady,' I said. 'In the first place, that sounds about right, doesn't it? I can't imagine keeping either one of them some-place they didn't want to stay. And in the second place, they escaped into the swamp. They know the swamp.'

'Not that part!' Echu Matta objected. 'That part is very dangerous!'

'Nobody took them,' Rothschild interrupted. 'That's what I was trying to say. My people had their eyes on the place constantly. No one came anywhere near that shack. The kids . . . they were just gone.'

'And you're absolutely certain they were there in the first place?' I asked him.

'My agents had the house under surveillance the entire time.'

It was odd to me that the FBI would let criminals take children and put them in a shack, but I held off on that suspicion.

I just stated the obvious. 'They escaped on their own. Let's go out there and look around.'

'No. We need John Horse!' Echu Matta railed. 'Where's John Horse?'

'OK, OK,' I told her. 'He's coming into the bus station today, if I remember the bus schedule correctly. Let's go there and find out when, exactly, OK?'

I could tell that she really needed to see the old guy. Rothschild stared at Pan Pan.

'Who's this?' he asked me.

'My cousin,' I told him. 'Twice removed.'

Rothschild started to say something, but he was interrupted.

'John Horse!' Echu Matta shouted.

It was startling to hear a woman who had been so calm under such a variety of circumstances suddenly louder than the Fourth of July.

I sighed. 'Let's go.'

And I climbed back into my car. Pan Pan hadn't moved.

'I'll wait for you here,' he told me. 'FBI freaks me out.'

I nodded.

Echu Matta and I got into my car. As I backed out of my parking space, a big FBI van pulled right up behind me.

We headed for the Fry's Bay Greyhound station.

TWENTY

The station was empty when we got there – like, Apocalypse empty. No customers, no stationmaster, no busses.

Instinct made Agent Rothschild pull his gun. We found the stationmaster dead behind the counter.

Rothschild stared down. 'Lively little town you've got here.'

'You hit us during a particularly busy season,' I told him. I rummaged around on the desktop where the stationmaster should have been sitting and found a schedule. It took a second to figure that the bus from Oklahoma City wasn't due until later in the day.

The stationmaster smelled like cigars. He'd been shot twice in the ticker, and there wasn't as much blood on the floor as there should have been.

'Ordinarily in a situation like this,' I said, 'you'd call the cops. But my thinking is that the cops did this, although I can't figure why, exactly. So, I'm calling the hospital. They'll collect the body and maybe even order an autopsy.'

Rothschild nodded. 'Collect the bullets. See if they match a police revolver.'

'Right.' I turned to Echu Matta. 'If your kids escaped into the swamp, that's where we should be. Not waiting here in a bus station for John Horse to come home.'

She was staring out the front window. 'I just thought he'd know what to do. I don't know what to do now.'

You could see that all the steam had gone out of her. It was kind of a miracle that she'd lasted that long, kidnapped, starved, hauled halfway across the country – and all by an ex-husband. No wonder she ran out of gas.

'You should go back to my place,' I told her. 'I'm going out to find your children. With any luck at all, I'll have them in my living room by the time you wake up. OK?'

She turned a half-vacant gaze my way, and then nodded. Then she wandered out of the bus station and was gone.

'I'll never understand them, the Seminoles,' Rothschild said when she'd gone. 'And I'm still trying to figure you out.'

'Let me know what you turn up,' I said. 'In the meantime, I'm none too happy with you and your FBI chums. You seem to have lost two little children. Two little children for whom I am personally responsible, both job-wise and promise-wise. So, you're going to take me, in that ridiculous black van you've got, out to that cabin where the crooked cops were holding them. And then you and me and whoever else is out there, we're all going to get our suits messy wandering in the swamp until we find them. Any questions?'

I could tell that about a hundred things went through Rothschild's mind before he settled on the perfect retort.

'OK.' He put his gun away and headed for the door.

I didn't move.

'I gotta call the hospital,' I said.

'You can call them from the van,' he told me, shoving me out the bus station door.

The cabin at the end of Blake Road was barely standing. Part of the roof was caved in; all the siding was loose or gone. Three guys in cheap suits were standing around in the gravel smoking cigarettes when we pulled up.

Before we were out of the van one of them started talking.

Rothschild held up his hand. 'I don't want to hear it. You know who this is?'

They all stared at me as I climbed out of the FBI-mobile.

'*That's* the Child Protective guy?' one of them asked, looking me up and down.

'He found the kids' mother in Oklahoma, along with all the other missing women,' Rothschild snapped. 'You know, the women that you three have been trying to find for half a year? How long did it take you, Mr Moscowitz?'

'About four days, if you include the drive time,' I answered him.

'So, shut up and tell him what happened,' Rothschild concluded.

The guy hesitated, since shutting up and telling me were, as they say in mathematics, mutually exclusive.

'All I really want to know is how long the kids have been gone from this house,' I said after an uncomfortable silence.

'Can't be more than two hours, tops,' the guy said. 'Hard to keep track out here. It's *really* humid.'

The other two just looked down at the ground.

'Go on,' I encouraged the talker. 'What happened?'

He blinked. 'What do you mean?'

'I mean something *happened* to make them skedaddle,' I told him. 'My sense of those two is that they don't do anything without a reason.'

'Oh. Well. Nothing *happened*, but about two hours ago, the girl started yelling that her mother was back. Any idea what she meant?'

I looked at Rothschild. 'I would say that's about when I pulled into town with Echu Matta in my passenger seat.'

'Spooky,' he said, without the slightest hint of spookiness. Because he didn't take it seriously, I presumed.

'Right.' I made a little dab in the dirt with the toe point of my shoe, and then drew a half circle around it to the south. 'This dot is the cabin; the crescent is a seven-mile half radius. They went into the swamp; they didn't go back to town or up to the highway. They think they can hide out in the swamp and then double back to town when it gets dark so they can get next to their mother. That's why the five of us are going to fan out in that direction.' I pointed toward the first of the cypress trees.

'Seven miles?' Mr Talker complained. 'That's a lot of ground for little children to cover in just a couple of hours.'

'Yeah, they're stronger and faster than you are,' I told him in no uncertain terms. 'And they know these swamps like you know your favorite booth at the Pancake House. Believe me, they could be ten miles away by now.'

'Listen,' Rothschild added, 'you keep calling out that you're helping Foggy Moscowitz. They'll trust that name, got it?'

They all nodded.

'Call the boy Duck and the girl Sharp,' I told them. 'That might help too.'

There was a big show of sighing and crushing out cigarettes, but the three guys eventually took off.

'By the way,' I called after them, 'you should just reconcile yourselves to the fact that you're going to mess up your suits.'

No one responded. Maybe their suits weren't as important to them as mine was to me.

I looked at Rothschild. 'I'm still adjusting to your alter ego, here. I was comfortable thinking of you as the new local dick.'

He sighed. 'I hate undercover work.'

'You seemed to get a lot of fun out of calling me "Jew-boy".'

He laughed. 'If I told you how many times I'd been called that – to my face – in the FBI *offices*, no less. Probably just releasing a little pent-up something-or-other.'

'Yeah.' I only took a second to meditate on the fact that in my old criminal world I'd never been called that.

'So, let's go.' He started toward the cypress trees.

'Hang on,' I said. 'Here's the thing: you stay on my right, and don't lose sight of me. I mean it. Lost in a swamp is the worst kind of lost there is.'

He nodded, and off we went.

Now, the first time I was in the swamps around Fry's Bay, I was in a slightly more hospitable part, owing to the fact that it was the part where a whole lot of Seminoles lived. This part where Agent Rothschild and I were, that was another story. It was less open, more tangled, and about twenty times more dangerous. It wasn't just the reptiles, including gators which could eat you in five bites, and snakes of all kinds that could bite you dead. There were also puss caterpillars – they looked soft, but if you got a bristle from them stuck in your finger, you'd be throwing up for hours and should really get to a hospital – and poisonous trap-jaw ants, brain-eating amoebas and sometimes black bears. Any one of them could put you down. And that was if five hundred mosquitoes didn't bite you and give you some godawful disease or just drive you crazy itching yourself to death. Give me a mob war any day.

Except for the fact that Sharp and Duck were out there somewhere and I had to find them.

It was easy enough to stick to solid land at first, but after twenty minutes or so, we had no choice but to wade into water up to our knees. And it wasn't just water. It was ooze and slime and bugs and slippery bottom.

The vegetation got thicker and the sunlight battled the canopy. Ferns, pepper trees, greenbrier, and the slime just kept getting worse.

Then, because God thought that making me ruin my shark-skin suit wasn't enough, he put the song 'Chloe' in my head. And not the beautiful Louis Armstrong version, the insane Spike Jones interpretation. Over and over again: 'I'll roam through this distant swampland, searching for you.'

Then: 'Hey, Moscowitz!' Rothschild shouted. 'I–I'm in a little trouble here.'

I glanced his way and saw when he meant. He was in water up to his chest.

'Are you stuck?' I asked him.

'Yeah, and I think I got a snake over here.'

'Don't thrash around, OK?' I said, heading toward him. 'You're in a boggy place that maybe is sucking you in. I know you don't want to, but you should try to go down on to the surface of the water and, like, swim out. Swim toward one of those cypress tree roots. That's where I'm going. I don't want to get stuck too, right?'

'Right,' he said, but his voice was shaky.

I sloshed toward the three cypress trees closest to him, but as I got closer, the water got deeper, so I circled around. When I got close enough, I could see he was in real trouble. I looked around for something to hold out to him, a low branch or a fallen tree limb. No luck. And he was making no headway trying to swim out of his predicament. He wasn't more than four or five feet away from me, but it didn't look like he was going to make it, and I knew it would be wrong for me to go after him.

So, what else could I do? I emptied my pockets. I took off my suit coat. I took off my pants. I tied one leg of the pants to one arm of the coat. And I called out to Rothschild.

'Hey! Heads up!'

He floundered and sputtered; came up coughing and gasping for air.

'What?' he demanded irritably.

'I'm tossing you this – it's a lifeline, see?'

He squinted, then nodded. I tossed. It fell short. I tossed again. He took a deep breath and lunged forward, just barely grabbing the cuff of my pants.

'Now kick your feet like you're swimming!' I yelled.

He did. I pulled. He inched toward me. I was nervous that the suit would tear. But Manny made a solid suit and it held together. Slowly but stupidly, I managed to land a Jew from the FBI.

And just as he grunted and swore his way up on to the little patch of land where I was standing, a voice behind me called out, 'Jesus, Foggy, what the hell are you doing in your underwear in this part of the swamp?'

I turned around to see my old friend Philip, Seminole strongman the size of a tank. He was dressed in a flannel shirt with the sleeves cut off and jeans that were smeared with swamp schmutz. His face was sweaty and his hair was wild.

'Hello, Philip,' I said, straining for dignity. 'I was just saving this poor schmo's life. How about you?'

'My mother sent me to fetch some hog plum and salt bush,' he answered softly, 'and I got lost. I was *really* happy to hear you guys.'

Philip was a great guy, sometimes muscle for John Horse, sometimes worked for Maggie Redhawk's brother. And he was a Benny Goodman fan, which marked him down on the positive side of my book right away.

I was already working on untying my pants and coat; Rothschild managed to sit up.

'Look, Philip,' I said, 'I'm actually out here looking for Echu Matta's children. They're roaming around somewhere in the vicinity.'

'Well, that's no good,' he said. 'This part of the swamp is dangerous. What're they doing out here?'

'On the run from the cops,' I said.

The full story could wait. Philip would understand about being on the lam.

'That way back there is the end of Blake Road,' I went on, pointing. 'Not very far.'

'Oh. Now I know where I am. Good. Want me to help look for Topalargee and her little brother?'

'I really do,' I answered.

'All right. Just a second.'

Philip turned around in a full circle, taking everything in. He looked up into the sky, then put his finger to his lips.

'There's other guys out here,' he whispered.

Rothschild stood up. 'They're with me.'

Philip nodded his head once. 'We should go this way.'

And he headed off east.

Rothschild got to his feet. 'You traded your home in Brooklyn for *this*?'

And there was that feeling again, about what was *home*. Because I had a second of wanting to speak up for Fry's Bay. Very confusing.

We followed Philip into the darker part of the swamp, and things got very humid. My clothes were soaked and had no hope of drying, which added to the delight. Every once in a while, I had to swat a mosquito or wade in ooze, but for the most part it was a better pathway than I would have found on my own.

Suddenly Philip stopped.

'What is it?' I whispered.

He pointed. It took me a minute to see what he saw. Black bears. Three of them. They were big, at least four hundred pounds, and swamp bears could be very mean. *You* try wearing a fur coat in that kind of heat – see if it doesn't make you irritable. They ate mostly plants, but they were also fond of small deer – the ones about the size of the two kids.

'I don't like that there's three,' I whispered.

'What is it?' Rothschild said, a little too loud.

I turned to him.

'Big black bears,' I said softly. 'They eat people. So, pipe down, OK?'

His eyes widened.

I turned back to the bears. They were scanning the area, sniffing. I figured they smelled us. A Florida black bear can smell a squirrel's buried nuts at a hundred paces, so I was pretty sure they could smell me, ripe as I was.

'They know we're here,' I said to Philip, to confirm.

He nodded. 'But they don't care. They got something else in mind.'

He pointed again, this time upward. And there, not fifteen feet away on a high branch of a cypress tree, sat Sharp and Duck. I had no idea how they got up there – there weren't any low branches. The bears were trying to figure that out too. They were at the bottom of the tree.

Sharp saw me first.

'Hello, Foggy,' she called out very calmly.

Her voice carried, even though it was a little thin.

The bears sniffed.

'You seem to have gotten yourself in a spot,' I told her.

The bears turned my way, but they were more interested in tree snacks than in three large men.

'Is that Philip?' she called out.

'Hey, kid,' Philip mumbled. 'If we distract the bears, can you shimmy down the tree?'

'We got up here,' Duck sang out. 'We can get down.'

'I don't care for the concept of distracting the bears,' Rothschild said.

He pulled out his service pistol.

'Don't do that,' Philip snapped, irritated. 'If you shoot them with that tiny little gun, they'll just get pissed off.'

'He's right,' I said. 'Put that away.'

Rothschild was reluctant, but he holstered his gun.

'So, what *do* we do?' he asked.

'There's three of us, three of them.' I sighed. 'If we make ourselves look as big as possible and go at them, we might scare them off.'

'*Might*,' Philip emphasized.

'Christ,' Rothschild snarled, 'I was safer stuck in the muck.'

'Well,' I sniffed, 'I'm really tired and I don't feel like standing around in the swamp, so I'm going to take a run at the bears and hope for the best.'

Philip picked up a nearby branch. I looked around for one too. Rothschild stood there trying to decide where he was. 'Is it possible that I actually died back there in the swamp, and this is hell?' he asked me.

'We don't believe in hell, right?' I answered.

'Yeah,' he said, 'but what if we're wrong? This would be a pretty good argument for it, this situation here.'

I looked at Philip. 'I always imagined that FBI guys would be a little tougher.'

Philip shrugged. 'He's out of his element.'

And with that I was snapped into a sudden awareness: I wasn't as much of a fish out of water in Fry's Bay as I used to be. There I was, a Jew in a swamp, and it didn't seem that odd to me at all. I had an impulse to thank Rothschild for helping me to understand that. But it passed when one of the bears roared. It sounded like a jet engine.

'Come on,' I said with a distinct air of fatalism.

We ran. Philip was howling like a dog. I was making some kind of yodeling noises that I didn't quite understand, and Rothschild was cussing like an outraged porn star.

The bears turned our way.

One stood on its hind legs. The other two lowered their heads and roared, showing us their teeth. I was on solid land but Philip was ankle deep in slime. We were closing in on the bears at a good clip, but it wasn't exactly frenzy.

Then, without warning, the bear on his hind legs lurched forward. I thought he was going to attack Philip, but instead it fell flat on its stomach, writhing and gurgling.

There was a very large knife stuck in the back of its neck, hilt deep.

I glanced up at Sharp.

'I'm gonna want that back,' she said.

'Why didn't you just do that before now?' I asked her.

'Didn't know which one was the leader until he stood up. They don't usually come in threes.'

The other two bears were confused. One of them sniffed the fallen leader. The other looked around like it was lost.

Rothschild froze and I dropped my tree limb.

Then I realized that Philip was singing. It was a soft song, but it somehow filled the air all around us. After a second, the kids in the tree joined in. The song was like friendly bees in the air all around us: humming, soothing, sweet.

It had an effect on the bears. One of them sat down, sighing. The other one continued looking around, lost.

After another couple of bars, I recognized the tune. It was something that John Horse had sung to me when I'd first met him and he'd dosed me with his hallucinogenic tea. It was a hypnotizing song. Even without the tea, it was very soothing.

As soon as Philip got close enough, he looked the seated bear right in the eye.

'Go on, now,' Philip said gently.

And that bear blew out a breath and got up – wandered off like it forgot something.

The other bear saw the situation – one dead, one leaving – and it didn't want to be the last one around, so it took off too, in another direction.

Sharp and Duck were already making their way down the tree, gripping it with their elbows and knees.

'What the hell just happened?' Rothschild muttered, looking around.

'John Horse,' Philip said.

And I knew what he meant. John Horse taught Sharp to throw a knife. And he taught Philip how to sing the song. Even when he was miles away, it was John Horse to the rescue.

Sharp sauntered up to the dead bear. It had stopped twitching. She pulled her knife out and wiped it on the bear's back.

'It's possible that the other two will come back to eat this one,' Philip began. 'They mostly eat plants, but this might be too much for them to pass up.'

'Meaning we should scram,' Rothschild said.

'What's he doing here?' Duck growled.

'It's a lot to explain,' I answered, 'but here's the big news: I found your mom; she's safe and waiting for you in town.'

'I *knew* it!' Sharp said, mostly to herself.

'And the cops who took us aren't . . . I'm confused,' Duck said, staring at Rothschild.

'This isn't Brady,' I told him. 'He's undercover FBI, trying to find out what happened to all the women, including your mother.'

Duck continued staring. 'You're right. It's a lot to explain.'

'I'm sorry, kid,' Rothschild said, and he meant it.

'Come on,' Sharp said, taking my hand. 'Let's go!'

'Man, is your mother ever going to be glad to see you,' I said. 'By the way, you should still be in the hospital.'

'No,' she said, pulling me forward. 'I should be with my mother.'

TWENTY-ONE

When we got back to Fry's Bay, I found that someone had brought my car back to the parking lot, but my apartment was empty. No sign of Pan Pan. I couldn't quite figure out what to do next. My brain just stopped working. Apparently, days without sleep will do that to a person.

'Christ!' I said. 'Am I ever going to come to the end of this thing?'

Luckily, Sharp knew what was what.

'You're about to fall down,' she told me. 'Why don't you go in your bedroom and do just that?'

I blinked. 'I gotta . . . The whole gig was to get you and your mother together.'

'You just told me on the ride here that you went to Oklahoma to get her,' she said. 'She's here, I'm here; it's just a matter of time before—'

My front door burst open, interrupting her thoughts.

John Horse stood in the doorway, filling the frame.

'Foggy!' he gasped.

'You're back,' I said, only a little deliriously.

'There's a dead guy at the bus station,' he said.

'I know.'

'And you're here with Brady,' he went on.

'Only he's not Brady, he's Rothschild,' I mumbled.

John Horse stared.

Rothschild took over.

'Mr Horse,' he said, holding out his hand, 'Special Agent Meyer Rothschild, FBI.'

John Horse didn't move.

Rothschild lowered his hand. 'I know it's a lot to take in. We've been after the men who were taking the Seminole women for half a year. Mr Moscowitz – and you, I guess – have helped us to solve the case. We're going to want to interview you and the women you've just brought home, of course . . .'

'The women are gone,' John Horse said calmly.

'I have to see my mother,' Sharp began, panicky.

John Horse looked at Sharp and said, '*Apockse, hachapitsalakin.*'

She nodded. Duck sighed.

Rothschild looked at me.

I shrugged. But I knew those words: *noon, tomorrow.*

Then John Horse smiled at me. 'I can see that you're just about to pass out, Foggy. Why don't you go fall down on your bed?'

I grinned stupidly. 'That's just what . . . just what . . .'

Sharp took me by the hand and pulled me toward my bedroom.

I don't remember anything after that.

I woke up and it was night. I was still in my suit and the curtains were closed. The apartment was silent. In my first conscious moments, the previous couple of days had a dream-like quality.

I sat up. Did I really go to New York? To Oklahoma? Did I really meet Pody Poe? And what about that bastard officer Brady?

I stood up. I stumbled to the living room. It was empty. Good.

I made it to the kitchen. Coffee.

Odd. The French press was ready, and the kettle on the stove was just waiting to be heated. I couldn't think. Just held a match to the gas. Poof: fire.

I stared down at the kettle until it whistled. I poured the water into the press, waited, pressed.

Coffee: good.

I managed to get myself, the press and my cup to the kitchen table all at the same time.

I sat.

The blinds to the sliding doors were open, and I could see the moon reflected on the water through them. Black water, silver moon; silence.

Before I knew it, half the coffee was gone and I was feeling a little more coherent.

The clock on the kitchen wall said that it was 2:17, but I could see that the second hand wasn't moving. That's why it was so pleasantly dark and quiet: my power was out. I got to the front door; opened it a crack. Everything was dark. Everything was quiet.

I had a momentary eerie sensation that I might be dead, but it passed right away. I couldn't have been a ghost. I smelled too bad.

What to do? Middle of the night, all alone, power out; midnight dreary.

Then suddenly there came a tapping.

I turned. John Horse was at the sliding doors, peering into my kitchen. I closed my front door and locked it before I went to let him in. I had the creeps for no reason I could explain.

The sound of the glass door sliding open was like thunder.

'Hello, Foggy,' John Horse said, not coming in. 'Looks like you got a little sleep.'

I nodded. 'What the hell is going on with the power?'

'It's out all over town.' He stared into my eyes.

'Why are you looking at me that way?' I asked him.

'I'm just trying to remember if things were this odd in Fry's Bay before you came to town,' he said, concentrating, 'or if it's always been this strange.'

There was a moment of silence.

'What's the verdict?' I asked him.

He shook his head. 'It's a funny little town.'

He stepped inside.

'I'm a little fuzzy about things,' I told him. 'Did you say that the women we rescued from Oklahoma are *gone*?'

'Gone back home,' he said. 'Into the swamp. Just didn't want that dick Brady to know what was happening.'

'You know that Brady is really Rothschild, FBI.'

'I know that a rose by any other name would still have thorns.'

I smiled. 'You have a skeptical attitude about anybody in the government.'

'I do,' he said. 'Can I have some coffee?'

I nodded. He poured.

'I keep thinking we're at the end of the slope,' I told him, sitting at the kitchen table. 'And then something else happens.'

'A lot of unanswered questions,' he agreed.

'I mean about getting the kids together with their mother, for God's sake.'

He smiled. 'Don't worry about that.'

'There's other stuff.' I only mentioned three. 'Who's the dead body in the bay? What was Icepick thinking? Why couldn't the FBI figure out in six months what it took you and me a couple of hours to crack?'

'Who killed the stationmaster at the bus depot?' he added. 'And why?'

'And where, by the way,' I concluded, '*are* the children I'm supposed to be taking care of?'

'They're fine,' he said. 'Maggie Redhawk took them over to Yudda's.'

'Yeah, about Maggie.' I set my coffee cup down. 'I gotta talk to her brother.'

Maggie Redhawk's brother was, among other things, one of the richest Seminole men in the country. Oil, banking, stocks – a tycoon with a ponytail. A very measured man, too. Patient. He knew how to wait. For instance, he'd been waiting since before he was born for the United States Government to live up to certain treaty promises it had made with the Seminoles in Florida. Waiting since 1866.

John Horse nodded. 'You borrowed money from him. To pay off the man in Oklahoma.'

'I generally stopped trying to figure out how you know stuff,' I told him. 'But how did you know that?'

He shrugged, which was the usual answer I would get from him on such a subject.

'OK,' I pressed, 'so are you going to tell me why the kids have to wait until noon tomorrow to be reunited with their mother?'

He looked down. 'There might still be owl people. It's too dangerous.'

I sighed. 'Look, I know that a lot of your Wise Old Man

shtick is for show, and you do it to impress me. But the guys who kidnapped those women are just crooks, plain and simple. And this guy, Bear Talmascy, he's just a crumb, that's all – a bad ex-husband. The world's full of them.'

He shook his head. 'I'm not talking about Bear. His spirit left his body a long time ago. He's not a human being any more. But he's not an owl person. He just looks like one. He's nothing more than a collection of bones and thoughtless action.'

'Then . . .' I began.

'I'm talking about the dead body in the county morgue,' he went on. 'The one that they thought was your friend, Mr Washington. *He's* a genuine demon.'

It was good to see the kids horsing around in the back booth at Yudda's. And there was Pan Pan. All three of them laughing. I realized what a rare commodity laughter had been for a while.

John Horse and I waved. The kids got out of the booth and ran to me. They both hugged me. Also a rare commodity.

'What's all this?' I managed to ask.

Sharp looked up. 'You saved our mother.'

'We were just too freaked out about being up a tree and scared of a bear to do this yesterday,' Duck concluded.

'Pan Pan is funny,' Sharp said, looking back toward the booth.

'He's a scream,' I acknowledged. 'I just don't know what he's doing here.'

'I came here after I dropped your car off,' Pan Pan said. 'I was hungry.'

'He's been telling us all about you,' Duck said.

I glared at Pan Pan.

He blinked. 'Not *all*.'

'Let's go,' I told him. 'You and me got work to do.'

He nodded and slid out of the booth. That was the thing about Pan Pan: even after all this time we'd been apart, he knew what I was talking about without my talking about it.

'Where are you meeting up with the kids' mother?' I asked John Horse.

'She knows where,' he said, voice lowered. 'And I'll stay with them until it's time to go see her. You go on and do your work.'

I couldn't be sure, but he seemed to be genuinely concerned about these owl people. Or was he still trying to play a part?

'Where to first?' Pan Pan wanted to know.

'Well, as long as you're in town, how would you like to see the sights?'

'Such as?'

'Such as the richest Seminole in America,' I told him.

'OK.'

That was all. Within the next ninety seconds we were in my car and on the way to the only building in Fry's Bay designed for the very wealthy. It was a snooty Art Deco number right downtown. If Mister Redhawk was in town, that's where he'd be. He owned the building and lived on the top floor, in the penthouse.

I parked my car in front, advertising the fact that I was visiting. Anyone who really wanted to know would recognize the black 1957 Thunderbird.

As we were getting out of the car, Pan Pan said, 'You've really kept this thing in great shape. I remember when you brought it in to me. Used to be baby blue.'

I encouraged him to save the reminiscences for a rainy day, and held the front door to the building, into the lobby.

He whistled at the marble excess. The marble echoed back.

We were up the elevator and into the foyer of Redhawk's digs before Pan Pan spoke again.

'Are you sure we're supposed to be here?' he whispered.

Swank made him nervous.

'Is that you, Mr Moscowitz?' a voice called.

It was Redhawk. He knew it was me. So why was he asking?

As soon as I rounded the corner of the foyer and got a gander of his living room, I got my answer. There was Watkins, with two burly Seminole gentlemen in classy suits, all pointing guns – some at Redhawk, some at me and Pan Pan.

'Gentlemen,' I said to the silent assemblage, 'this is certainly an unexpected state of affairs.'

'You messed me up real bad,' Watkins said. He sounded exhausted.

I picked out one of the Seminoles.

'*Leech-as-chay*,' I snarled at him.

He took a second to register surprise that I spoke his language, and then gathered up a small portion of bravado. 'You're not going to kill us.' He laughed, nervously.

'*Nakin chief ka teh?*' I demanded.

'What's my name?' another guy asked. 'Kiss-My-Ass, that's my name.'

'John Horse sent us,' I told the assemblage.

At that the Seminoles grimaced like I hoped they would. The mere mention of John Horse's name could sometimes freeze blood.

'He sent us to take revenge,' I told the strangers, 'because we're immune to the Owl People. This man standing next to me? He's already dead. His name is Pan Pan Washington.'

'The guy who got dumped in the bay?' one of the Seminoles asked Watkins.

'He's just trying to make you nervous. That's not—'

'You've been taking Seminole women,' I interrupted, louder. 'You've been shipping them to Oklahoma. Watkins has been helping you with the technicalities: picking out the women here in Fry's Bay, cinching their disappearance with the hotel, keeping it all hushed up with the police.'

'He–he doesn't know anything,' Watkins stammered, trying to assure his cohorts.

I took several steps closer to him; Pan Pan did too.

'The Seminole Nation of Oklahoma gets federal money based on population,' I said. 'Bear Talmascy figured out a way to make money by counting these extra people as members of the Oklahoma congregation. It's a variation of an old Social Security scam. Only with this thing, there's proof: you *have* more people there in Oklahoma – these Florida Seminoles. And then after that you also *dispose* of the women, to collect their tribal death benefits. Two scams for the price of one.'

'There's probably more money in selling the women,' Redhawk corrected me.

'Yeah,' I snapped. 'I don't really want to think about that.'

'We're going to start shooting in about five seconds,' Watkins raved, 'unless Redhawk gives us money and a way out of town.'

Out of the corner of my eye I could see Pan Pan shift his feet. It had been a while, but the last time I saw him do that, he was getting ready to pull out a .44 and start shooting.

'Pan Pan,' I said calmly. 'Show these men your driver's license.'

Without batting an eye, Pan Pan whipped out one of his many licenses and flashed it.

'Pan Pan Washington,' he said. 'Shot in the head and dumped in Fry's Bay.'

That little bit of distraction handed me the opportunity I wanted. I kicked high enough to knock loose the gun in Watkins' hand. Redhawk took care of the next move – he shoved his fist into Watkins' face so hard that blood spurted out of his nose in two directions.

Pan Pan had his .44 out, popping off two clean shots. One into a Seminole kneecap, the other into a different Seminole gun hand.

I stomped sideways on Watkins' foot and rapped his throat with my knuckles. He went down like bag of sand, messy all over the nice marble floor.

Pan Pan had the tip of his pistol at the temple of one of the Seminoles. I took the gun away from the other one.

'How long have these guys been here?' I asked Redhawk.

'Don't know,' he answered. 'I came home about fifteen minutes ago and they were here, waiting for me.'

'I came to say thanks,' I began.

'Where are the children?' he interrupted.

'They're OK,' I assured him. 'John Horse is with them, taking them to their mother at noon.'

'No,' he said. 'Watkins told me. Bear Talmascy is here. In Fry's Bay. He's lost his mind. He's going to kill *everyone*.'

TWENTY-TWO

That's why Watkins and crew were so crazy to get out of town: Bear Talmascy. And they *were* crazy to go to Redhawk for help. In the first place, if they hurt him, there wasn't a cave on earth where they could hide from Seminole retribution. In the second place, Mister Redhawk would rather kill those guys than help them.

Or maybe that's just how stupid Watkins was. Because screwing with Seminole citizens in a place where Redhawk *and* John Horse lived, that was significantly stupid.

It was clear that Bear Talmascy would be looking to settle the score with me and his ex-wife – and probably even John Horse. Was that why John Horse acted so strange about the kids being reunited with their mother? Did he somehow know that Bear was coming?

I looked at Pan Pan. 'We should get back to Yudda's.'

'I can take care of these things,' Redhawk said, staring down at Watkins. 'You should go; be careful. Bear Talmascy is not entirely human.'

'We've met,' I said, heading toward the elevator. 'I'd still like to talk about the money you put up to pay off Pody Poe.'

'Let's see if we're both alive tomorrow,' Redhawk said softly. 'Then maybe we'll talk.'

In that jolly mood, Pan Pan and I headed back to Yudda's.

'I like those little kids, Foggy,' Pan Pan said after a second or two. 'Could you drive faster?'

I eased the accelerator forward and the T-Bird jumped. When we drew closer to the waterside and Yudda's shack, we both saw an ominous black column of smoke rising into the sky. I put the pedal all the way down and jumped out of the car as soon as we were next to the restaurant. It was entirely hidden by the smoke.

I cracked open my trunk and hauled out an industrial-sized fire extinguisher – something that had come in handy on more than one occasion.

I ran to the front door and doused the entrance.

I yelled, 'Yudda!'

No answer.

There was no way to see if anyone was trapped there, so I had to go in. I could hear Pan Pan yelling at me from behind, but I didn't understand what he was saying. I just charged, coughing and spewing extinguisher foam everywhere.

The place was the inside of a furnace thanks to the tin roof. Something on the griddle was on fire. Smelled like rancid grease and rotten coleslaw. I sprayed it down and eased toward it, still hot as a blowtorch. My eyes were stinging and I was having trouble breathing, but the fire was going out. Didn't help the smoke any; in fact, it made it worse. But I used a napkin from the bar to fan away the smoke from my face; it looked like the place was deserted.

I emptied the extinguisher all over everything in the cooking area and then backed out of the joint.

Pan Pan was at the door. He'd found a hose somewhere and was watering down the doorway and the tin roof. The roof crinkled and complained, but it was relaxing.

'Nobody inside,' I panted.

'Man, you are one crazy Jew,' Pan Pan swore. 'What the hell did you think you were doing?'

'I didn't think about it,' I admitted.

He shook his head. 'You are *way* too invested in this job you got here.'

'You said you liked those kids,' I protested.

'I do,' he told me. 'But this is a three-hundred-dollar suit!'

I set the extinguisher down and stared at Yudda's building. 'You know what this means, don't you?'

'No idea.' He turned off the hose. 'I guess it could mean that this Bear Talmascy guy's been here.'

'Bear Talmascy? I left him tied up in Oklahoma waiting for Pody Poe.'

'I don't know,' Pan Pan told me. 'But they all say that Talmascy is a real badass.'

I sucked in a breath and shouted, 'Yudda!'

Nothing for a second, and then coughing.

'I hope you done called the fire department.'

Yudda's voice was coming from the docks. The smoke was drifting high and wild. Didn't really think a call to the firemen was necessary. I headed for Yudda.

He was lying on his side in a pool of blood, a huge kitchen knife in his hand.

I got to him and knelt down.

'Shot twice,' he gasped. 'Stings like a bastard but it's mostly fat that got hit.'

I managed to untie his apron and get it off. Tore it in two and stuffed wads of it into his gunshot wounds. Then I looked around.

'Where is everybody?' I asked.

Big fire, gunshots, people yelling – where was the hoi polloi? Not a soul in sight.

Yudda grunted, and then painted me a picture. John Horse and the kids were sitting in the back booth at Yudda's, waiting for noon. Yudda was making sandwiches for them – Muffuletta Po'boy with Bayou spread, lots of horseradish and tobacco.

All at once a sky-blue Cadillac Deville barreled up to the docks and a demon from hell exploded out of the driver's seat. Bear had a gun in each hand and he just started shooting. People scattered. Bear was screaming.

John Horse grabbed the children and flew out the back exit, a rusted strip of corrugated tin on hinges in one corner. Yudda grabbed his carving knife and stood in the doorway, hunkered down.

Bear busted in and shot Yudda without saying a word. Yudda stabbed Bear in the stomach twice before Bear shot Yudda again. Yudda fell backward and landed on the floor with a pounding thud.

Bear roared, 'Where's my children?'

But Yudda looked dead. Bear kicked him. Then Bear howled like a dog and set Yudda's place on fire.

With that, he got back in his car and screeched away.

Yudda crawled out of the burning building, headed for his

boat at the dock and the telephone that was in it. He made it about halfway there, and then Pan Pan and I showed up.

'Very succinct,' I told Yudda.

'If you ain't gonna call the fire department,' he grumbled, 'could you at least call me an ambulance?'

But right on cue: sirens.

'Where did John Horse and the children go, man?' I asked Yudda.

Yudda took in a breath, opened his eyes wide and passed out.

I waited with him until the ambulance took him away. The fire truck had already quelled the worst of the smoke. Notably absent: Rothschild, or any cops. What had happened to Rothschild?

Pan Pan was doing his best to be invisible in between two storage sheds by the docks. I signaled him and we managed to slip back to my car unnoticed.

'Where to?' he asked, slipping into the passenger seat. 'We got to find those kids, Foggy. The Bear sonofabitch is crazy!'

'Well, John Horse can't get the kids back to the swamp fast enough,' I said, cranking the engine. 'That's where they'd be safest. But I wonder if he might try for the next best thing.'

And with that we were off.

The joint was deserted, as usual. A little over an acre of land: flowers, and shrubs and vines that had flowers, giant striped grass, a rock garden and tons of shade. There were three benches, all handmade, all facing the sea. It was a very quiet place, and always kept up, well-watered, tribally maintained. There was no sign or marker.

'What's this?' Pan Pan asked, a little irritated. 'A park?'

'Abiaka Park,' I said. 'Abiaka is as famous to Seminoles as Osceola.'

'Who?'

I sighed. 'Doesn't matter. Abiaka was a great spiritual leader. John Horse comes here sometimes to meditate. Me too. Sometimes.'

'*Meditate?*' Pan Pan closed his eyes. 'Jesus, Foggy. What the hell happened to you?'

'The point is,' I pressed on, 'that there's a little hiding place here that not many people know about. Come on.'

I got out of the car; Pan Pan likewise.

In the middle of the park, beside a big boulder, there was an ancient magnolia tree the size of a small house. The lower branches leaned on the ground and the leaves were as thick as a wall. Also smelled like heaven thanks to the blossoms.

But if you could manage your way past the branches and the leaves and you knew what to look for, you'd see that you could climb about halfway up the trunk to a treehouse, solid as a rock, built into the branches, nearly invisible.

'What the hell are we doing?' Pan Pan complained.

I put my finger to my lips and then pointed up. He still didn't see it. That's how good it was.

He stared, he squinted, then he shook his head.

'What?' he whispered.

'Up,' I whispered back.

I grabbed a handful of tree and hoisted myself up.

'This is a three-hundred-dollar suit!' he repeated.

I ignored him.

He said something; probably for the best that I couldn't hear it. Then he followed me up.

It was difficult, but a couple of minutes later, I put my hand on the platform of the treehouse.

'Do you think you could make any more noise?' I heard John Horse complain.

'It's Pan Pan,' I objected, out of breath. 'He's not as savvy about nature as I am.'

'Bite me,' Pan Pan managed to say.

I crawled on to the platform and sat up. I couldn't stand because of low branches. But there was John Horse, standing in the doorway. That's how big the house was.

Duck appeared, grinning.

'You climbed a tree in your suit,' he said.

I nodded. 'I'm glad to see you too.'

'Bear Talmascy,' John Horse began.

I held up my hand. 'I know.'

'Yudda . . .' he went on.

'Fine,' I assured him. 'We waited for the ambulance before I thought of coming here.'

'Bear Talmascy has lost his mind completely now,' John Horse said.

'He's on the run from the guys – from some not-very-nice people,' I said. 'He's not only insane, he's scared.'

John Horse nodded. 'The men who financed his scheme, they want their money.'

I stood. 'I made sure they got paid, so they wouldn't be after *me* – you and me, for messing them up. Um, Mister Redhawk.'

That's all I needed to say. John Horse understood.

'Well, come in the house and shut up,' he said. 'We're hiding.'

Sharp was asleep in a corner of the room, cradling her big knife like it was a rag doll.

Pan Pan scrambled up on to the platform then, cursing under his breath. When he saw the kids, he softened. A little.

'That man shot up the whole place, all over the diner and the docks and everything,' Duck began explaining.

That man. The kid didn't know that Bear was his father.

'Let's whisper now,' John Horse announced to everyone.

'What's your plan, exactly?' I asked John Horse. 'Hide up here until Bear dies?'

'So many people out to kill him,' John Horse answered. 'That shouldn't be too long. But just in case, I sent word to Philip. And to Echu Matta.'

I knew what that meant. Bear Talmascy wasn't long for this world. Because if Echu Matta saw him again, she'd obliterate him.

'Thanks for helping Philip out of the swamp, by the way,' he went on.

'He told you about that?' I asked. 'When?'

'I heard,' he said, not looking at me.

Sharp sat up then.

'Foggy?' she said sleepily.

I went over to her. 'Hey. Glad you got some sleep. I'm not convinced you should be out of the hospital, you know.'

'I wasn't sleeping,' she said very softly. 'I was talking with my mother.'

'You were dreaming,' I said tentatively.

'What's the difference?' she asked me.

'Don't you think it's kind of funny,' Pan Pan interrupted, 'that we're up a tree trying to get away from a bear? Like on *The Beverly Hillbillies* and stuff.'

I stared. Everyone did.

It was clear that Pan Pan was not reacting well to the culture shock, from Brooklyn to Fry's Bay.

Then it hit me. Pan Pan Washington was in Fry's Bay. That wasn't right. Like some kind of hallucination from some of John Horse's funny tea. Pan Pan was planted up to his nuts in Brooklyn. Excuse the expression. You could hardly get him to cross the bridge to *Manhattan* if there wasn't a girl involved. What the hell got him to come all the way to Florida? The whole rigmarole with the dead body in the bay? That would have got me a frantic call, not a visit. People out to kill him? He had a hundred places to hide. What in God's name made him take such a trip? I mean, the guy loved me, and the feeling was mutual, but that wasn't what brought him to my door.

But before I could go any further down that road, there were strange noises in the woods.

John Horse nodded. Everyone in the treehouse froze.

Could have been park visitors, but that would have been unusual. The real possibilities were Rothschild's federal agents, John Horse's Seminole mob, or Bear Talmascy and his lost mind.

I reached for my pistol. Pan Pan already had his out.

'Does Bear know this house is here?' I whispered.

'Did you?' John Horse asked me.

His head was tilted and he was grinning.

'Yes,' I told him. 'There's a girl.'

He nodded. '*Hachi.*'

'She told you.'

He shrugged. 'I heard.'

Another story for another time, but Hachi: pale blue summer dress, twice as smart as me, and a whole lot nicer – she'd brought me to the treehouse. More than once.

Then there were gunshots.

Then came the screaming.

'I know you're here somewhere!' Bear shrieked.
And he fired his gun again.
I looked at John Horse. 'He knows you're here?'
John Horse sighed. 'He could have followed us here. Or maybe Echu Matta told him about this place. Or maybe his owl nature gave him insight.'
'Baby!' Bear howled. 'Where are you?'
'Baby?' Pan Pan wondered.
I got it. 'He thinks his *wife* is here.'
'He drugged her, stole her, used her and sold her.' Pan Pan shook his head. 'And now he's calling her *baby*?'
'Why is that man calling our mother *baby*?' Duck whispered.
Sharp had roused herself and her knife was in her hand. 'He fell in love with her after he kidnapped her. He wants her to be his. He wants a family. But I know the stories.
'One story. *Once there was a bear. He had the biggest house there was, and everyone was jealous. It was a cave in the middle of the woods. But Bear needed a big house. He had a fine wife; he had two children.*
'*They were very happy in the house. They did everything together. They ate together, they laughed together, they slept together.*
'*One night there came a knock on their door. It was loud. They all got up. They opened the door.*
'*Standing there was Skunk. He bowed.*
'*"I was just passing by," said Skunk, "and I noticed what a mess your house is. Through the window."*
'*The bears looked around. Their house was a mess. But they were bears. Large bears. What could they do?*
'*"I could use a nice warm place to sleep," said Skunk. "I will be your housekeeper. I'll keep your home neat and tidy, if you'll just let me sleep in the corner."*
'*Bear thought. It would be nice to have a tidy home.*
'*"All right," said Bear. "Come in."*
'*Never let a skunk into your home.*
'*The instant that the skunk was in, he turned and lifted his tail. He sprayed Bear with his poison.*
'*Bear howled. He sneezed. He coughed. He ran from the home. He ran and ran, trying to outrun the smell.*

'Then Skunk looked at the rest of the bear family.

'"Take off," said Skunk, "or I'll do the same to you."

'Mother Bear gathered up her children and left. She didn't follow her husband. Now Skunk has the biggest house there is.

'Another story. When the world began, Bear owned Fire. Bear kept his family warm on cold nights, and had light when it was dark. Bear carried Fire with him wherever he went.

'But one day, Bear and his family came upon a place where the ground was covered with acorns. Bear put Fire down so he could gather acorns to eat. The acorns were sweet and crisp, better than any other food Bear had ever eaten. Bear began to roam, eating the wonderful food. He went farther and farther away from Fire.

'Fire was happy enough at first, sitting on the forest floor. But as the sun went down, its wood was gone, and it began to sputter and smoke.

'"Help, Bear!" said Fire. "Feed me or I'll die!"

'Bear was too far away to hear.

'But Man heard, trudging through the forest.

'"Help, Man," said Fire. "Feed me or I will die!"

'Man had never seen Fire before, so he asked, "What do you eat?"

'"Feed me wood!"

'So, Man gathered sticks and gave them to Fire. All at once Man was warm. All at once Man could see in the night.

'The next morning Bear came back. But Fire was angry with Bear.

'"You abandoned me!" said Fire to Bear. "I almost died! Man saved me. Go away. I belong to Man now!"

'Then Fire blazed up white, so hot that it drove Bear and his family away. His wife left him for being so careless, and took the children with her.

'And now Fire belongs to Man.'

Sharp concluded her stories.

'Bear gave his home to Skunk, and abandoned Fire when it needed him most,' she said softly. 'Bear doesn't get to *have* a family.'

TWENTY-THREE

Meanwhile, down below in the park, the commotion had continued. Bear was thrashing.

I was staring at Sharp because I didn't quite understand why she'd chosen to tell us Seminole stories in the middle of gunshots. Sure, she was a strange one. And maybe she'd been having weird dreams before she woke up. But it seemed like something more, like some part of her knew that Bear was her father.

Then I realized I'd gone back to thinking of her as Sharp instead of Topalargee. Maybe it was the same reason certain people nicknamed me Foggy: because they liked me. Sounds like a description but it's really a term of endearment.

More gunshots. This time bullets ripped through the leaves close to our treehouse.

'Sorry,' I said to no one in particular. 'I'm going to have to go take care of this guy once and for all.'

I headed for the door.

'No!' Sharp whispered harshly. 'That man will kill you!'

'Foggy . . .' Pan Pan began.

John Horse had a different response. He grabbed my arm and wouldn't let go.

I smiled.

'Is this where you told Echu Matta to meet her children?' I asked John Horse.

He squinted, then nodded.

'Right,' I went on, 'so the thing is I promised to reunite these kids with their mother. And if this moron shoots her, that can't happen and I'll be a welcher. Am I a welcher, Pan Pan?'

'Foggy,' he said again.

'So, you understand, I really am going down there to explain things to Bear.'

I shook off John Horse's grip and motored for the door.

'Stop him,' Duck said to his sister.

'No,' she told him. 'He's right. He has to go. He's the only one who can stop the bear.'

Out of the corner of my eye I saw Duck nod, suddenly understanding.

'Like when we were up the tree,' he said. 'He ran at the bears then, too.'

And suddenly Rothschild's fear took hold of me: that we'd died in the swamp and now we were all trapped in some kind of weird hell where Jews attack bears.

But it passed.

I was out the door and on to the platform before the next bullets tore through the leaves.

'Bear!' I shouted. 'Stop shooting. I'm coming down.'

There was a heartbeat of silence. Then: 'Who the hell is that?' he called out. 'Where are you?'

'It's Foggy Moscowitz. You know. The guy who found you in Oklahoma.'

He fired three more shots in the direction of my voice.

'If you kill me,' I told him patiently, 'I won't be able to tell you where Echu Matta is.'

Another heartbeat.

'I'm reloading,' he warned.

But he didn't shoot.

I got down the ladder, my gun in my hand but down to my side. I looked around.

There he was, hair wild, eyes bloodshot, face as red as cherries.

'Look what you did to my sharkskin suit,' I told him.

He was breathing hard, like he'd been running, but he managed to snarl, 'Where's my wife?'

I shook my head. 'You don't have a wife. You let a skunk take over your house.'

I didn't know why I'd said it. Maybe just to be spooky, maybe to see if he knew the story. Didn't matter. It had consequences.

Bear busted out crying. 'You think I don't know that? You think I'm stupid?'

'I think you did irreversible damage to your spirit.' The

Seminole shtick seemed to be working; better than swapping bullets.

'I–I was trying to get my family back,' he said, a little desperate. 'That's all I wanted. I wanted to find my wife and my children.'

'By kidnapping and selling the women?'

He shook his head so hard it hurt the air around it. 'No! No! That wasn't me!'

I stared at the sweat on his face and the look in his eye. And then I realized what had *really* stolen the Seminole women. The red face, the breathing. Bear had a coke habit. A long one, and a bad one.

'I can get you some help,' I began.

But that wasn't what he wanted to hear. He growled, aimed and fired.

The bullet zipped past my ear.

I dropped, then shot.

I got him in the thigh. I thought that would make him stop and think.

It didn't.

He unloaded his gun in my direction. Luck and salty eyes made his aim bad. I only got hit once, left forearm.

I stood up and looked at his empty pistol. 'I don't want to shoot you any more, Bear,' I said.

He lowered his head and charged, moaning.

All I had to do was take a step to the side and hold out my foot. It was like a vaudeville routine. He tripped, flew forward; found the ground with his face.

Then: a voice behind me.

'Don't kill him.'

Echu Matta emerged from the shadows on the other side of the magnolia. There was a knife as long as a broom handle in her hand.

'I wasn't going to kill him,' I started.

But she was on top of him, knee planted in the small of his back. Her hair was tied behind her head and she was wearing a frilly white top with new red jeans. She'd dressed up to see her children. It was a strange sight to see when she raised her knife to chop off Bear's gun hand. It severed clean, right at the joint. But there was a lot of blood.

Bear was trying to make a noise but the pain stuck in his throat.

'You beat me,' she whispered. 'You beat our children; took our money. I was happy when you were gone. And then you came to *steal* me? Women died, in that storage container. My people *died* on the way to Oklahoma!'

'I wanted you back,' he managed to groan. 'I came to get you. It was for us. For the family. Get my family back. Together.'

'People say you're an owl man now,' she went on, ignoring his rambling. 'But you're just a half-man. Most of you is gone already. I'm going to enjoy taking the rest of you.'

With that she took hold of one of his ears and slowly sliced it away from his head; tossed it like a kitchen scrap.

That stirred him. Probably panic. He rolled, kicked, and Echu Matta flew off him. She landed on her back and Bear was up, looking for his gun.

'Bear,' I warned him.

He didn't seem to hear me. He kicked the knife out of Echu Matta's hand and it slid across the ground. Then he reared back his big foot again to kick the woman on the ground.

'Bear!' I fired one in front of his face.

Didn't stop him. He kicked Echu Matta in the head.

I shot him three times, once in the knee cap and twice in his side. He just looked surprised. He turned to me.

'What am I doing?' he asked me.

'Bleeding to death,' I said.

'Where are my children?' His voice was hoarse.

'You don't *have* any children,' Echu Matta grated.

'They were with that fat cook,' he insisted. 'I set his house on fire when he took them from me. And there was a Black Seminole. A ghost. A man I already killed once. In New York. Is he here?'

He dropped to his good knee, staring at Echu Matta.

'I wanted to get it back,' he explained very reasonably. 'I wanted the life we had before. When we were happy. I just needed a little money to make that happen. You have to understand that.'

'You were never happy!' she shot back. 'You have to be a human being to be happy, and you were never human!'

'I–I . . . was I an owl?' He blinked.

'No, Bear,' she snarled. 'You weren't anything. You weren't any good at being alive. And now you're going to die. That's all there will be to your story. Nothing and less than nothing.' She spat in his direction.

He looked around, like he was seeing the garden for the first time.

'It's pretty here.' He looked at me. 'What's that smell?'

'Magnolia blossoms,' I told him.

'Oh.' And with that he fell; thumped the ground like a fallen tree.

From up above my head, a little voiced called out, 'Is he dead?'

'Topalargee?' Echu Matta shouted.

'Mama!'

There was a scramble, and a rain of magnolia blossoms, and suddenly Sharp and Duck were all over their mother. The frenzy was so exuberant that they all landed on the ground. They were rolling and hugging and kissing and laughing and crying and talking and shouting and . . . happy. Because they were human.

Philip and ten or twelve other Seminoles, men and women, showed up not long after that. One of the women began tending to Bear, who was not, after all, dead.

I looked over at her. 'Are you taking him to the hospital?'

She looked up. She was one of the women I'd seen in Oklahoma, one of the captives.

'No,' she said serenely. 'I'm just patching him up so that he'll be alert for what we're going to do to him.'

The sweet voice made the horrible vision worse: what Bear had in store was something that made me a little dizzy to think about.

Then I noticed that Pan Pan was standing by my side.

'So,' he said with a certain air of finality, 'this is your job. I can see how you might get to like it.'

His head inclined toward the mother and child reunion. I caught his eye. 'Not quite finished yet,' I told him.

'You're not? What's left?'

'In no particular order,' I began. 'Who killed the stationmaster? What happened to the other cops? What's happening with Watkins? And probably first and foremost: why did Icepick kill some guy in Brooklyn, give him your ID, and then drive him all the way to my front door? Or – and here's the weirdest wrinkle of all – did Bear just say that *he* killed the guy?'

'Oh,' he acknowledged. 'That.'

'The guy in the morgue?' John Horse said.

He was standing right behind me, even though I hadn't heard him come up.

'You know who that is?' I asked him, turning around.

He nodded. That's all.

'Are you going to tell me?'

He shook his head.

'Why not?' I asked.

'Tribal matter,' he said.

'*What?*' I stammered.

He whistled to everyone. Silence descended.

'Let's go,' he told everyone softly. 'Gather up Bear. We should be gone before the FBI men get here.'

With that the entire contingent of Seminoles, including Echu Matta and progeny, were gone.

I turned back to look at Pan Pan. 'Tribal matter?'

TWENTY-FOUR

P an Pan and I also managed to be gone before the FBI showed up, if they ever did. But as we were driving back to my place, my brain began to work the way it was supposed to.

'The guy in the morgue,' I said, eyes on the road, 'was a Black Seminole.'

'You said that,' Pan Pan agreed.

'That's what John Horse meant when he said it was a tribal matter.'

'Sounds right.' Pan Pan nodded.

'But, see, John Horse has what you'd call an expanded notion of the word *tribe*.'

Pan Pan looked at my profile. 'I don't follow.'

'For example,' I explained, 'he considers the Jews a tribe. Which we kind of are.'

Pan Pan shrugged. 'OK.'

'And what's a tribe, really, but an extended family, right?'

He nodded. 'I guess.'

'Which would make you and me,' I said pointedly, 'members of the same tribe.'

He didn't have a retort to that.

We pulled into the parking lot at my apartment. I turned off the engine and sat there. Pan Pan didn't move. He was waiting.

'What did you think of the kid's stories about the bear?' I asked, staring straight ahead.

'Spooky,' he answered.

'Yeah,' I agreed. 'Then let me tell you another one. What I think happened with Icepick, and why Bear thinks he killed *you*. It begins this way.'

Not long ago, I explained to Pan Pan, Bear Talmascy stood in the shadows in a corner of LaBracca Pizza. He had just proposed a crazy idea to equally crazy hoods. Take Seminole women from Florida to Oklahoma by census time, report the increase in the population, collect the government subsidy and then sell the women. Profits! He kept mum on the Social Security scam he also had in mind. That was his own personal gravy. The hoods were impressed. Not especially with the scheme, but with the cold-bloodedness of its progenitor. They didn't know from Seminoles, they only knew that the Indians were like the blacks: disposable. Not a bad way to make money. So, they agreed to finance the operation, with the understanding that they would double or triple their expenditure for transport, gun support and connections for the 'distribution' of the women when the gig was done. Bear hooked up with Watkins, a partner in the scam, and they began rounding up the women. Only something happened. One of the Cherokee men working with Bear, or maybe with Pody Poe in Oklahoma, didn't have a taste for the whole thing and got into it with Bear, or Poe, or some bigwig in New York. Whatever, that guy had to be taken care of, so they called on Sammy 'Icepick' Franks. The problem was Icepick. Even though he was a stone-cold killer, he had ethics. He did the job, iced the guy but he didn't like it, and he wanted to make it right. After he bopped the guy, he somehow got Pan Pan Washington's ID. He shoved it into the stiff's pocket, snorted a couple of bags of coke and flew down the coast to Fry's Bay. He knew that would get me involved and I'd set matters right, because that was my rep.

I concluded my little tale by turning to Pan Pan and staring a hole in his eyeballs.

'How'd I do?' I asked him.

He nodded. 'Just about a hundred per cent.'

'How'd Icepick get your ID?'

Pan Pan wouldn't look at me. 'He asked. He's not a guy you tell *no*.'

'He's not,' I agreed. 'But there's more to it than that.'

He nodded.

'Are you going to tell me?' I asked him.

'I am,' he said slowly, 'but I don't know how you're going to take it.'

I sat back in my seat. 'I'm pretty tired. I don't really have the energy to beat it out of you.'

'Like that would happen.' He sniffed.

'But you're going to tell me anyway,' I went on, looking past my apartment building at the ocean, 'because that's the reason you're here. The real reason. To tell me something.'

'Yeah.' He let out a long, slow breath. 'They want you back, Fog. The guys. The Organization. They want you back in Brooklyn.'

And there it was: the thunderbolt.

It took me a minute to get to my first question.

'Why?'

'I think maybe you got a whiff of the idea,' he began, 'when you visited LaBracca's yourself. You didn't sense a certain air of, maybe, respect?'

I thought about it. While I was thinking, he went on.

'Some of these guys, including Eddie "Two Shoes" Hicks – they worked it with the cops. Your record is, like, erased.'

'How do you mean?' I still wouldn't look at him.

'OK, so why did you leave Brooklyn in the first place?'

'You know why,' I told him. 'Corner of fifty-third and twelfth after midnight.'

'Go on,' he said. 'The whole spiel.'

'It was a 1967 Ford Mustang Fastback, red on red, with silver wheel wells,' I said softly. 'I mean, who parks a car like that on the street in that neighborhood? I pulled out the old rod and hook toolkit, and in no time I was sitting behind the wheel. I fired it up, I eased it into the street, I turned on the lights. Then came the yelling and the screaming and I saw, in the rearview, two people chasing me. I floored it and the Mustang flew away.'

'But there was something in the back seat,' he said.

I nodded slowly. 'A kid, maybe a year old – he began bawling up a storm. Scared the hell out of me. I just jumped out of the car, left it in the middle of the street and beat it into the alley. Ended up in Prospect Park by the lake. I don't remember much about the rest of that night.'

'But a couple of days later, you heard the story.'

'Yeah.' I closed my eyes. 'Some dame was cheating on her rich husband – with a deli clerk, no less. She left her fourteen-month-old kid in the Mustang. That was her and the clerk

chasing after me. The cops found the car and the kid right away. The car was fine; the baby was asleep.'
'That wasn't the problem.'
Why was he making me say the whole story out loud?
'No.' I took in a deep breath. 'The mother had a heart attack while she was chasing me down. She didn't make it. And when the rich husband heard the whole story, including the deli clerk, he ditched the kid. Said it wasn't his. Let the deli clerk take care of it.'
'And the cops?'
'Yeah,' I concluded. 'They put two and two together. Who else in that neighborhood would steal such a car but me? They stop me on my way home from Temple, and before I know it, I'm in handcuffs in the back of a squad car, headed for Grand Theft Auto, on account of the Mustang was a pricey item. The thing is, if you can pop a lock on a snazzy car, handcuffs don't mean much, so I took them off, jimmied the back door of the squad car, and was out on the street before the cops could get through the first stoplight.'
'And here is where you ended up. In Fry's Bay.'
'Yes, atoning for my sins by taking care of wayward children.' I sighed. 'Go ahead. Make fun.'
He shook his head. 'I'm not making fun. Not by a long shot. And neither are the guys in the Organization. That's why I wanted you to tell your story. I wanted you to feel it again. I wanted you to understand that the guys in the Organization, they want you back. You're some kind of hoodlum hero. You're – I kid you not, Foggy. You're good PR.'
Good PR. Funny to think of everything I'd done in Fry's Bay as a publicity stunt.
'Icepick wanted your ID,' I nodded, 'because it was a sure way to get *me* involved. He didn't know that I'd already be involved because of the kids.'
'Right.'
'But he wanted me to be involved because of his *ethics*.'
'Right.'
'So, what's in it for you?' I asked Pan Pan.
His shoulders sagged a little, and I could see, out of the corner of my eye, his face turn sweet.

'Are you kidding with that?' He shook his head. 'I get *you* back. Back with me in Brooklyn.'

'So, it's a win all around.' I put my hand on the door. 'The Organization gets good PR, Icepick feels like a hero, and you and me are *you and me* again.'

I climbed out of the car.

Pan Pan got out and followed me to my front door. 'So?' he wanted to know.

'So . . . it's a lot to think about,' I told him.

'What's to *think*?' he snapped. 'Come home!'

I opened my front door. 'Yeah,' I said. 'I've been having a lot of conflicting feelings about just that idea lately.'

'What idea?'

'The idea of what's *home*,' I said, stepping into my apartment.

TWENTY-FIVE

I didn't remember much after that. I was tired again, and the wound in my forearm was bothering me. The bullet had only grazed, but that's not like you see in the movies. It really hurts, and it saps your energy. I patched it up, but then I passed out and didn't get back up until the next day, mid-morning. I'd slept in my suit. It was a mess. I tossed it into my dry-cleaning bag and stumbled into the shower.

And all the time in the shower, something was bugging me. Something about Bear. Couldn't quite get it clear. It was just outside the edge of my mind.

Robe and slippers, into the living room: Pan Pan was gone. I was alone in the apartment. Five eggs and half a loaf of toast later, I got into the light blue seersucker, the two-tone wingtips, and headed for the police station.

The station was overrun with strangers: FBI guys, I figured. Agent Rothschild was sitting at his old *Brady* desk. There was more noise and more activity in the room than I had ever seen. And not a local in the bunch.

Rothschild looked up. He hadn't slept, and his clothes looked like the inside of a dumpster.

'Where have you been?' he asked me.

'Unconscious. And what do you care?'

'I have questions.'

'What makes you think I have answers?' I stared.

'Then what are you doing here?' he pressed.

'Yeah.' I looked around the familiar station house filled with unfamiliar faces. 'What *am* I doing here?'

'Well,' he sighed, 'the whole thing is pretty much settled. Bear Talmascy cooked up a scheme to make money off his own people, his own family, as I understand it. He got financial backing from some guys in New York. And I have a feeling you know the guys, because why else would this body of your friend turn up in the bay here in Podunk-Ville?'

'You haven't figured that out yet?'

'Not my gig,' he answered. 'I'm here for the group kidnapping thing. Still, I am curious.'

'As I understand it, curiosity can only do you harm,' I told him. 'But unfortunately, I also have questions.'

'About?'

'Bear Talmascy is a lot of things, but smart enough to figure all this out? That's not one of them.'

'You think someone else came up with the kidnapping/census/Social Security scheme?' He nodded. 'I'm afraid I agree. Certain people are talking about the guy. He thought that he was somehow going to get back together with his wife and kids. He's half-crazy.'

'You could say that.'

'Yeah.' He gave me the eye. 'Any idea where he is?'

'Part of it was the drugs,' I said, ignoring his question. 'He had a bad coke habit. But part of his *crazy* was that he thought he was a supernatural creature, which was reinforced by the fact that a lot of people in his family thought that too. But when I woke up this morning, I had a nagging feeling about Bear.'

He squinted. 'Yeah. Me too. Wonder if it's the same feeling.'

I shook my head. 'I'm still adjusting to you being a good guy – and a Jew – instead of the *khnyok* you used to be.'

'FBI training. Most people find it easier to play opposite of type, they say. Plus, it's supposed to throw off suspicion.'

'It certainly got you in with Watkins.'

'That worthless piece of trash,' he mumbled.

'Where is he now?'

'Oh, we got him,' Rothschild said. 'Since he's a party to a federal crime, he and his bunch are on their way to Tallahassee. State Capital. Wait for trial there.'

'And it's your opinion,' I guessed, 'that he wasn't the mastermind behind all this either.'

'He couldn't mastermind his own lunch order.'

'Agreed. So, who?'

He stood up suddenly. 'You want to go talk to Bear?'

'What?' I stared. 'You got *him*?'

'Found him near that dockside diner,' he told me. 'People

said he set it on fire. He was shot up real good. Talking out of his head.'

I couldn't figure why John Horse had done that – left Bear in town. But he had.

'Where is he?' I managed to ask. 'Where's Bear?'

'He's chained to a bed over at the hospital.'

Rothschild headed for the door. I followed.

The hospital was busier than usual. Maggie Redhawk rolled her eyes when she saw us coming and motored our way.

'Somebody has to come in here and deal with that blister of a human being!' she told us before she got to us.

'Meaning *Bear*,' I assumed.

'If he's not crying he's singing,' she went on. 'At the top of his lungs! And chanting about – he scared away two candy-stripers. He told them to open the window because he was about to turn into an owl and fly away!'

'So, you're not among the faithful,' I interrupted, 'who believe that he can do that.'

'Not in the middle of the day!' Maggie snapped back. 'Has to be moonlight.'

'Give him a sedative,' Rothschild suggested.

'We did,' she growled. 'Twice the legal limit. And he's still singing and crying.'

I nodded and headed for the room. 'We'll see what we can do.'

Rothschild followed.

When I got to the door, Bear tried to sit up. His left hand was handcuffed to the bedpost and his right arm was immo-bilized by a cast. His face was bruised and swollen. His head was bandaged.

'Foggy?' he mumbled. 'Is that you?'

'Mr Talmascy,' Rothschild began.

'I don't want to talk to you!' Bear roared. 'You lied to me! You're not a crooked cop at all. You're an FBI!'

'Bear,' I said.

'You gotta help me, Foggy,' he told me, still trying to sit up. 'You gotta tell my wife and kids: I just wanted to get them back. That's all I was trying to do.'

'No, it wasn't,' I said. 'You were trying to make money.'

'To get back my wife and kids!'

'Topalargee told me two stories about the bear who didn't deserve to get his family back. It wasn't ever going to happen.'

'The bear who let the skunk in the house,' Bear said.

'How long did you live in Oklahoma after you left Florida?' I interrupted.

Bear relaxed. His head hit the pillow. 'Five years, I guess.'

'And in those five years you came to work for Pody Poe.'

'Yeah.'

'How long you work for him?'

'Three.'

'And you talked a lot about your family back in Florida.' I shot a look to Rothschild. 'And then one day, he started talking to you about this scheme with the women here in Florida.'

'Not Poe,' Bear said sleepily. 'The other guy.'

He squeezed his eyes shut. It looked to me like the tranquilizers were finally beginning to take hold of him.

'What other guy?' I asked. 'Someone from New York?'

'There were guys from New York there, sure,' he mumbled, eyes closed. 'You know that one: Icepick.'

'Icepick was there when you were talking about taking women from Florida for the Oklahoma census?' Rothschild jumped in.

'Uh-huh.'

'But it wasn't Icepick's idea,' I said.

'No, I said: the other guy.' Bear was almost asleep.

'Some other guy from New York?'

'The old man. The rich one. From Okla—'

And that was all we were going to get from the guy. He was out. Too bad. I still had questions about Icepick.

Rothschild stared down at the poor unconscious sap.

'Somebody from Oklahoma came up with the thing?' he finally asked.

I weighed my suspicions, thought about it twice and then let out a sigh.

'I should have known,' was all I said.

And then I headed for the door.

*   *   *

I was out on the sidewalk and headed back to my apartment before Rothschild caught up with me.

'Where are we going?' he wanted to know.

'I'm going back to my apartment,' I told him. 'I don't know where you're going.'

'You're done for the day?'

'I didn't say that.' I picked up my pace. 'I walked to the police station this morning; I'm going to get my car.'

'This afternoon,' he corrected. 'It's afternoon already.'

'OK, but I still need my car for where I'm going.'

'Bear said something that . . . What did you mean when you said, "I should have known"?'

I stopped walking.

'Look,' I said to the guy. 'I still have residual suspicions about you, left over from your time as *Brady* – the racist dickhead. It was a role you played with a lot of *oomph*. Even De Niro's not that good an actor. There's something off about you. For example: you tell me your name is Rothschild and you buddy up to me thinking we have some king of Hebrew Brotherhood, but we don't. My primary religion is Brooklyn. My current life is based on atonement. Yom Kippur. So, unless you have some FBI juju to slap on me, shove off. I'm going to my apartment to get in my car to take a drive to clear my head.'

I stared into his eyes all the way to the back of his head. He blinked first.

'Will you at least tell me who it is,' he said, 'once you've found out?'

'Found what?'

'Who actually came up with this whole kidnapping scam.'

'Oh.' I started walking again. 'Probably not. I work for Child Protective Services, not the FBI. Do your own work.'

I kept walking and he didn't follow. I figured I made him just mad enough – or curious enough – to put a tail on me. At least I hoped he would, because I didn't relish the idea of driving my T-bird into the swamp all by myself.

TWENTY-SIX

First, it's a paved road, then a dirt path, and eventually a winding, overgrown trail leads to John Horse's home in the swamp. It took about an hour and a half if you drove the whole way, or an hour if you parked when the trail started and walked the last couple of miles. The FBI tail stayed way behind me, but there was no hiding the fact that they were there. It was a single-lane road in the middle of nowhere, no other cars and no place to hide.

I parked my car on a little pad of ground where I'd parked before, and where my friend Philip sometimes parked his Jeep. The feds found a shady spot before a bend in the road and tried to look invisible.

I got out, locked the T-bird, even though I didn't need to, and started the trek.

Right away I regretted wearing the old two-tone wingtips. I liked them, and they were going to suffer.

Guys I knew in Brooklyn paid a hefty monthly fee to belong to a gym where they could sit in a room that was half as steamy and humid as the trail to John Horse's house. I hadn't walked a hundred yards before the seersucker was soaked and my lungs wanted to be gills.

I could hear the FBI guys behind me, but I couldn't see them when I turned around. They were probably pretty good city guys. But my few years in Florida had taught me that nothing you've learned in the city prepares you for a swamp.

When I hit the five-way split in the trail, I stepped off the path entirely, up on slick moss and dead palmetto for a few yards, and then back down on to the path. They'd never know which of the splits to take. I wanted them nearby, but not on top of me. Of course, there was always the possibility that they'd get lost and be eaten by alligators.

Another sweltering half-mile, and John Horse's little slice of heaven came into view. I always thought about the line from *Little Big Man* when I looked at the place. 'I see the dump – where's the village?'

A scattering of naked cinderblock houses in random order sat in various stages of disrepair. John Horse had the nicest one, but that was a little like saying, 'This is the scab that bothers me least.'

There was smoke coming out of the window, which meant he was cooking something. Otherwise, the whole settlement looked deserted. I knew better, though. There was always a sentry. Somewhere in the shadows were a couple of armed guards. I kept my hands visible and my face smiling. They knew me, but that wouldn't keep them from shooting me if I looked squirrely.

I made it to John Horse's door without seeing anyone, but I had the itchy feeling of eyes on me anyway. I didn't have to knock. The door was open and John Horse was sitting on the floor in front of his little wood burner next to the window.

'Come on in, Foggy,' he said without looking up.

'I assume you knew it was me since I parked my car.'

He nodded. 'And I assume you know you were followed here.'

'FBI,' I told him.

'I made you some *sofkee*,' he said.

Sofkee was a drink made of corn. Not exactly a soup, more a beverage, and it wasn't bad. John Horse had made it for me before. It went good with turtle.

'You knew I was coming *before* I parked my car, then,' I told him.

'I knew you would figure it out,' he said, still not looking at me. 'I thought it would be today.'

He got a pot holder and poured two mugs of the *sofkee*. He gave me the mug that said, *There's plenty to see wherever you go in Florida!* He took the one with the hand-painted flamingo.

I knew better than to try to talk before I sat down on the dirty floor and took a sip of the stuff. Deep breath, apology to the pants and cross-legged on the floor, I drank. Burned my tongue a little. Experience had taught me to wait for him to speak.

He took a few slow sips, closed his eyes, enjoying the taste, and swallowed. After a minute or two, he set his mug on the floor next to him and finally looked me in the eye.

'Tell me.'

I put my mug down. 'Tell you how much I already figured out, or how much more I want to know?'

'Both.'

'OK.' I folded my hands in my lap. 'You say you're the grandfather of Echu Matta, and I'll go along with that. You sent her children into Fry's Bay to look for me, not her. You knew what happened to her. But you also knew that a Seminole investigation wouldn't get you what you wanted. It had to be me or somebody like me.'

He laughed at that. 'There's nobody like you, Foggy.'

'I get that a lot,' I admitted. 'It's not usually a compliment.'

'In this case it's just an observation,' he said.

'So.' That's all I said.

'You want to know if *your* observations are right.'

I nodded.

'Echu Matta is my granddaughter; her children are my line. I began to notice women missing from the job at that fancy hotel.'

'The Benton,' I interrupted.

'But they were taken to distract me from what was really happening,' he went on.

'Which was?'

'You know.'

'I think I do,' I said. 'Someone talked Bear Talmascy into this ridiculous scheme; fed his broken brain with the promise of putting his family back together. He had no idea that the real goal was to get to you.'

He closed his eyes. 'Do you think these things through, or do they just come to you?'

'I'm not sure I know what you mean by *these things*,' I told him. 'But this thought started in the shower this morning.'

'I never took a shower. Maybe I should.'

'The point is who would steal women, use them for a relatively petty sum of money, and then dispose of them in some hideous way, just to get at you?'

'Think of the way you had to sneak into New York,'

he began. 'Then triple that, and you have the way I had to sneak into Oklahoma.'

'You didn't sneak into Oklahoma,' I objected.

'It didn't occur to you why I went to Eddie Harjo?'

I blinked. 'That's right. You're John Horse. People in Oklahoma know who you are. You could have rallied the troops just as well as he did. Better, maybe. But if he did it – I mean, even if people thought they recognized you, they wouldn't say it was you. It was too improbable. You stay here, in the swamp. In Florida.'

'Like you do.' He nodded. 'Which is why we got out of New York as fast as you could drive. You didn't even call your mother, let alone go see her. Which I know you wanted to do.'

'Right,' I said. 'Let me see what I get if I add two plus two. Some rich or powerful person in Oklahoma – not a Seminole, maybe someone in government – has a grudge against you. It's got to be a mighty grudge to have such a complex machine and such collateral damage. Some person or persons initiated the scheme to call you out.'

He smiled. 'But what they didn't reckon on was you.'

'Which is why you used your alleged great-grandchildren,' I said. 'To get me hooked.'

'I didn't use them,' he objected. 'Their mother was taken. They were involved.'

'But you sent them to Fry's Bay to get to me.'

'Oh.' He nodded. 'Yes, I did that. They didn't want to involve anyone outside the tribe. They thought they could do it on their own.'

I laughed. 'I think the chances are pretty good that they could have done it on their own, if either one of them could drive.'

He picked up his mug and finished his *sofkee*. It was time for another moment of silence, so I finished mine too. Sweet, still hot – the kind of concoction you were supposed to be suspicious about, especially with a character like John Horse. On more than one occasion he'd dosed me with some kind of Mr Toad's Wild Ride.

'There's nothing in it,' he said softly, reading my face – or my mind.

'Too late anyway,' I told him. 'It's gone. Good.'

'Yes.' He set down his mug. 'Good.'

I waited.

'A long time ago,' he said at last, not looking at me, 'I was supposed to be taken to Oklahoma. We all were. All Seminole boys were shipped to the Seminole Oklahoma reservation. It was a ploy by the American Government to unsettle us, keep us disoriented, take us from home and "properly socialize" us.'

'But you didn't go.'

'I kept a lot of us from going. We hid out in the swamp. We sabotaged the trucks that were supposed to take us away. We started a war on the police and, after a while, the US military was called in. This was a long time ago.'

'You said.'

'But a man, an American soldier, a captain not much older than me, was killed. It was an accident, but his family blamed me, because I was the instigator of the confrontation. My legend, in their family, is not a good one.'

I took a deep breath. 'His family is from Oklahoma.'

He nodded.

'They – let me guess,' I went on. 'They're oil-rich, snake-mean, shit-kickers, and they've been out to get you for a long time.'

He nodded again.

'They really did invent this stupid money-making scheme of kidnapping Seminole women just to get you?'

'Well, they like money.' He shrugged. 'And this is only their most recent attempt to hurt me. They failed again, because they're wrong. They always fail.'

'That's what makes them so mean,' I said. 'A crazy husband and an affable hood like Pody Poe, they can't hold a candle to a rich guy with a grudge.'

His eyes agreed, but before he could add to his story, dogs were barking and men were shouting.

'Ah.' He stood up. 'They're here.'

'Who's here?' I asked, scrambling to my feet and pulling out my gun.

'Put that away, Foggy,' he said, glancing at the pistol. 'No need for it, and I don't want you to get hurt. I'm going to need your help and I don't want you to get shot.'

I hid the gun just as two Caucasians in plain black suits busted into the room. *They* had guns.

'FBI,' one said.

'John Horse,' the other chimed in, 'you're under federal arrest and will now be taken into custody.'

John Horse didn't move a muscle. 'No, I won't. This Seminole land is an independent nation. You have no authority here. And technically, we're still at war with your country. You are enemy combatants, with weapons drawn, on foreign soil. I'll try to convince the people outside not to kill you. But it won't be easy if you start pointing your guns at them.'

I could see, past the agents and through the door, a dozen or more Seminole men and women with rifles. All pointed at the men from the FBI.

'You guys followed me here,' I said, 'on orders from Rothschild?'

They were too slow to respond.

'Oh,' I said. '*Not* Rothschild. Well, that makes me think better of him.'

'These men are directed, whether they know it or not, by the family we were just discussing,' John Horse told me.

'You guys are from the Oklahoma City office?' I said.

Before they could respond, John Horse whispered a name.

'Bill Hale,' he said.

'Bill Hale,' one of the FBI men echoed. 'Famous case. What about it?'

'Hale bribed and killed his way to wealth and a place in Oklahoma politics,' John Horse went on. 'Mostly by stealing the oil royalties from members of the Osage Tribe. Started in 1921, with an Osage woman named Anna Brown. She was found in a ravine. The undertaker found a bullet hole in the back of her head. She was just an *Indian woman*, so not much was made of it. Then her mother Lizzie died two months later, also suspiciously. But it wasn't until white oil men were also murdered that FBI agents were sent to help.'

John Horse had given his speech in a monotone, and without any facial expression. But it had an impact. On me, at least.

'One of the rich oil men,' I said to John Horse, 'was a member of the family who hates you. They developed a *relationship* with the FBI that long ago. That's why these guys are here now. Nothing to do with Rothschild or his investigation.'

John Horse nodded once.

I took one step toward one of the agents.

'My name is Moscowitz,' I began. 'I'm with Florida Child Protective Services. Might not mean that much to you, but I'm winding up an investigation that has federal implications.'

'We know who you are,' the man said, irritated. 'We're working with Rothschild.'

'Not now, you're not,' I disagreed. 'You're here for a completely different reason.'

He countered. 'We're here because this man, John Horse, is implicated in the case of kidnapping across state lines.'

'Implicated in the *kidnapping*?' I laughed. 'How?'

'Just stand out of the way,' he snarled. 'We're taking this man into custody.'

I shook my head. 'Here's the thing: there are around thirty guys behind you, all with guns. And other guys have already dismantled your car, or am I wrong?'

'You're not wrong,' John Horse answered calmly.

'And when you're dead, we'll all drag your bodies into the swamp and every last morsel will be alligator food, or am I wrong?'

'Alligators eat everything,' John Horse said.

'Or you can say, to whatever oil baron who *hired* you, that you couldn't find John Horse. And you can go home and try to resume your duties with the FBI, if you truly work for that agency. If you do, I'm going to make that very difficult for you. So. Dead or unemployed. Those are really your only options.'

To emphasize my point, a dozen or so Seminoles made their presence known right behind the FBI agents, rifle barrels grazing various creases in their cheap suits.

I held out my hand. 'Give me your guns. You're a whole lot safer if these men know you're unarmed. Otherwise, a sudden twitch or an unexpected sneeze could be mistaken, and *then* where are you? Alligator lunchmeat. Think about that.'

One of the FBI guys thought about it. The other fired his gun. John Horse stumbled, then dropped.

Then a couple dozen Seminole rifles exploded, and just like that there were two fewer crooked FBI agents in the world.

I ran to John Horse. There was blood all over his shirt. He wasn't breathing.

Before I could figure how I'd get him to the hospital, an older Seminole woman was pulling me away from him. I tried to shrug her off, but she was stronger than I thought. I glanced at her. She was Philip's mother, the one who made the great turtle soup.

'They shot John Horse,' I said, dizzy and stupid.

'I know.' She stared me down. 'But you can't be here. There is going to be trouble. FBI. You go on home now, Foggy. Go back to your car and drive home.'

A couple of the younger men got hold of me then, and I was ushered out of the house and halfway down the trail to the road before they let go of my arms. And then, without a word, they were gone.

I don't remember walking the rest of the way back to the car, but I guess I did. How else would I have ended up back in my apartment? I remember making coffee and gulping it down. I remember sitting at my kitchen table.

And I remember my front door exploding into my living room, and the FBI agents storming in like I'd busted up their hive.

Then I was conked in the back of the head and I don't remember anything after that, for a while.

TWENTY-SEVEN

When I woke up it was Tuesday. I only knew that because I asked. I was in a cell in the Fry's Bay police station. There were only two, and in the one next to mine there were three dead Seminole men. Or they looked dead. The station was very quiet.

'What the hell?' was my first question, which I asked lying on my side on a cot.

One of the Seminole men growled and sat up. So, he wasn't dead.

'Foggy?' he mumbled.

It was Philip.

I sat up. Took some doing.

'What day is it?' I asked him.

'What difference does *that* make?' he asked right back.

'I'm just curious.'

'Tuesday. Does that help?'

'Not really,' I said, rubbing my face. 'I don't know what day it was when I saw John Horse get killed and I got hit on the head from behind. So, I'm not really sure why I asked.'

Philip nodded sagely. 'That was yesterday. Monday. FBI came. Rounded up a bunch of us. Don't know when they brought you in, because they hit us on the head too. Hurts.'

'It does,' I agreed. 'I'm having trouble seeing.'

'They didn't get John Horse's body, though,' he went on. 'My mother took him into the swamp, to the other place.'

I knew what place he meant. John Horse had different hiding places all over the swamp, but there was one special hut, made from trees and vines, mostly. He told me, once, that it was his real home. The home for his spirit.

'Does that mean he's dead?' My voice sounded funny, like someone else was asking the question.

Philip shrugged and stared at the floor. 'I didn't think he *could* die.'

Before I could get philosophical, Rothschild appeared, and I stood up.

'If I'm not out of this cell in about three seconds,' I began before he could say anything, 'I'm going to figure a way to burn your house down with everyone you know inside it.'

'Or you could just get your friend Icepick to pay me a visit,' Rothschild countered.

'In the first place, he's not my friend,' I said softly. 'And in the second place, how would you know what he does for a living? And in the third: that's not a bad idea.'

'How do you know I'm not here right now to let you out?'

'Because I'm not as stupid as I look.' I smiled. 'I've been figuring this whole thing six different ways, but your guys messed up worse than you can possibly imagine. They killed John Horse.'

He shook his head. 'I didn't send those men . . .'

'Who else would put a tail on me?' I interrupted. 'You're working for . . . Wait. Philip? You happen to know the name of the family that's been after John Horse for so long? I should have asked John Horse, but we were interrupted.'

'Wilkins,' he said without looking up.

I glared at Rothschild. 'FBI on the Hale case a long time ago in Oklahoma, they got bought off by this Wilkins bunch. And then it morphed into an official FBI long-term case. Maybe you don't know the origins of it, maybe you do. No matter what, you're off my Christmas list because you came after John Horse. He's not somebody you mess with around here.'

'Listen to you,' he said. 'You sound like a local.'

Then it hit me.

'Wait,' I said to Philip. 'Why does the Wilkins name sound familiar?'

Again, Philip shrugged, *still* not looking up.

'They own the houses in Oklahoma,' I said, mostly to myself. 'The ones where Bear hid the women. It was this Wilkins gang.'

I could tell that the wheels in Rothschild's brain were spinning – you could smell the friction.

He was still silent when Philip finally looked up. And even when Philip lunged at his cell door, Rothschild didn't move.

Two seconds later, when the door swung open and Philip had Rothschild by the neck, it was too late. Rothschild's face was as red as a beet, and the rest of the Seminole men were out of the cell.

Philip tilted his head my way, his eyes still on Rothschild, and one of the other men came to my door. He shoved something into the lock and the door popped open just like that.

'Is it the best idea,' I said to Philip as I slipped out of the cell, 'to kill an FBI officer inside a jailhouse?'

'Because of him, John Horse is dead,' Philip answered reasonably. 'I don't care if he's called Brady or Rothschild or *hompusche*.'

I turned a sympathetic eye toward Rothschild. 'That last word? That means *breakfast*. He's implying that he'll take your body into the swamp and feed it to the alligators there, like they did with your cohorts. You made an impression as Brady. I thought it was just me, but apparently everyone hates you.'

He tried to speak, but Philip was squeezing his windpipe hard, and no sound would come out.

Then he made a very stupid mistake. He reached inside his coat, going for his gun.

Philip swatted him, backhand, across the jaw, and he was out the way Ali put down Foreman in Zaire. He was crumpled on the floor like leftover takeout food.

I checked his coat. There was a gun. I went for his ID.

'Well, what do you know?' I said to Philip. 'This guy really is FBI.'

'What do you mean?' he asked.

'I mean that he is, but the other guys, the ones who came to John Horse's house, they *weren't*.'

'So, who were they? Who did we kill?'

'Yeah.' I sighed. 'Let's figure this. The Wilkins clan, they want John Horse. They get Bear riled up, he thinks he's got a way to get his family back, make the Oklahoma locals some money: win/win. Only a guy called Icepick doesn't like what's going on. He's got a code. So, he pops one of the men who riled Bear but dumps him in our bay.'

'Bear was in this thing mostly to take the fall if anything went sideways,' Philip said.

I had to smile. 'You been hanging out with me too long. You're beginning to talk *Brooklyn*. But, yes, that's what I figure.'

Philip sighed. 'I'm going home now.'

Without another word, he and the other Seminole men split. I was afraid I knew where they were going. They were going to a funeral.

I didn't know what to do, so I went back to my office. Paperwork. It's better than gin at taking your mind off everything else. I had no idea how everything else would sort out, but I was going to fill out my forms. Children had been in danger. I found their mother and brought her home. Case closed. If the details got the attention of the *real* FBI or some other higher authority, that would be swell. But my work was done.

A couple of hours later I was just signing the last form, when who should walk into the office but John Horse. He was wearing a flannel shirt and jeans, construction boots, a baseball cap with no insignia on it, and a pair of new-looking horn-rimmed glasses. And he didn't look real.

'Hello, Foggy,' he said, standing in the doorway.

I nodded. 'Imagine my surprise to see you here. You were dead in the swamp yesterday.'

'I only die when it suits me.' He stepped in and set a very large tooth on my desk, right on top of my paperwork. 'That's from a panther.'

'Neat,' I said, staring at it. 'Large.'

'Was a big panther,' he told me.

'I wonder why his tooth is now my paperweight.'

'It's a gesture.' He smiled. 'You're an honorary member of the Panther clan. My clan. You helped me out and you protected my relatives. That makes you family. Sort of.'

I touched the panther tooth.

'Why not?' I said. 'You already tell people that we're related, your tribe and mine.'

'Oh, wait.' He shoved his hand in his right front pocket and produced about a dozen crumpled hundred-dollar bills and dropped them on to the table beside the tooth. 'In case you want something a little less Seminole for a thank you.'

He sat down.

He nodded.

'You know that those men in your house, the Wilkins bunch,' I said, 'didn't manage to get you after all.'

He nodded again. 'They failed one more time, thanks to you.'

'That's what makes them so mean, like I said.'

'That's what makes them so *persistent*,' he said, softer. 'They'll try again.'

'I'm sorry.'

He stood up.

'But this time, you helped. So, thank you for protecting my great-great grandchildren,' he said, turning to leave.

'Wait a minute, wait a minute,' I complained, coming to my feet. 'How is it you're not dead, really?'

'Oh, that.' He didn't turn around; kept his back to me. 'Well. I wasn't dead, obviously.'

'I saw you get shot. I saw the blood.'

'You never been shot before?'

'Once or twice,' I admitted. 'But I was young and I had a whole lot of coke in me.'

'I'm not so old as you think,' he said, and motored for the door to my office. 'And I have medicine a lot stronger than cocaine in my blood.'

'You're not going to give me a real answer, are you?'

'No,' he said.

'Then how about one last question, maybe?' I asked. 'Since I'm family now.'

He stopped just outside the door frame. 'What is it?'

'Just how old are you?'

'In human years?' he croaked, back still to me. 'I have no idea. I hope you like the tooth.'

'I do.' I glanced down at my desk. 'But you know I can't keep this money.'

I looked down and gathered the bills together.

But by the time I looked up again, seconds later, John Horse was gone.

I knew better than to go after him. I stared down at the panther tooth for a while. Then I reached for the phone and dialed long distance.

It rang for three minutes before Pan Pan answered.

'What?' he barked.

'It's me. I figured you'd be back in Brooklyn by now.'

'Oh. I *hope* you're calling to tell me when you'll be home,' he said.

'I'm calling to tell you to thank Icepick for me. Weird as it was, he did me a favor by dumping that guy's body in the bay down here.'

'Elrod Duncan.'

'Sorry?'

'The stiff's name was Elrod Duncan. He worked for a guy who worked for a guy.'

I nodded. 'Didn't look like an *Elrod.*'

'It was an alias. He couldn't very well go by his real last name.'

'Which was?' I asked.

'*Horse.* Can you believe it?'

It took me a second or two to get out, 'No.'

'Don't you know a guy down there who pretends to have that same name?'

God help me, I was suddenly suspicious of Pan Pan. I was suddenly afraid that he was looking for John Horse, like the crooked FBI or the Wilkins family.

And there it was: the switch. Whose side was I on? Who were my people now?

'That guy?' I told my old friend. 'I don't think he's real. They talk about him, but I think it's a made-up story.'

'No,' Pan Pan pressed. 'I met him. *That* guy.'

'Oh, *that* guy? He's a local nut-job. Total loon. Likes to call himself John Horse, but that's because he named himself after a famous Seminole who died in 1882.'

That much was true. There was a John Horse, also known as Juan Caballo and Gopher John. Imprisoned with Osceola when General Jesup, a stain on the American military, captured them under a truce flag. *That* John Horse escaped, hid out in the swamp, and successfully fought off the entire American army. Our guy in Fry's Bay was named after him. They say.

'I see,' Pan Pan said.

I wasn't sure what he thought he saw. I decided to make it clear.

'Hey, Pan Pan.' I sighed. 'Will you tell Icepick I said thanks? And tell my mother I said hello?'

'Sure.' I could hear him shaking his head. 'So, you're not coming home.'

'Yeah, nobody's more surprised than I am,' I told him. 'The thing is, see – I *am* home.'

He didn't say goodbye.

Later that evening, I took a walk down to the beach out my back door. Shoes off, pants rolled up, the whole thing.

The moon was up and the waves were small. There were little glowing things in the water, like bits of stars broken off, floating under the ocean before they burned out. Something came up out of the waves for a second or two. Could have been a dolphin.

I stared out, thinking of all the things about Brooklyn I missed: bagels from Izzy's, my mother's chicken, that smell of gasoline on asphalt. Then I thought about all the things in Florida that irritated me. It was too hot when it was hot; colder than you thought when it was cold. It was impossible to escape the smell of fish in the summertime. And not another Jew within a hundred miles. In any direction.

So why the switch?

When I was a child, I spoke as a child, I understood as a child, I thought as a child: but when I became a man, I put away childish things.

Maybe there, feet in the sand looking out at the moon on the ocean, I was on my way to becoming a man.

Or maybe it was this. On the tenth day of the seventh month you must deny yourself, because on this day atonement will be made for you, to cleanse you. Then, before the Lord, you will be clean from all your sins.

Was it possible that I'd finally been forgiven?